Endorsements for *Goodbye, Maggie*

Shortlisted, 2019 William Faulkner – Wisdom Competition

"*Goodbye, Maggie* is a wonderful story that can be read on several levels … In the entertaining style of his prior novel, *Hippies,* Gautier gives us characters we know in unique situations and keeps us smiling throughout."

Michael T. Tusa, Jr. Author of *A Second Chance at Dancing* and *Chasing Charles Bukowski*

Goodbye, Maggie

Goodbye, Maggie

Gary Gautier

Shakemyheadhollow.com press
637 N Hennessey St
New Orleans, LA 70119
drggautier@gmail.com

DESIRE
says the neon above the Royal Sonesta door on Bourbon

HUGE ASS BEERS
screams the street vendor's sign

HOMO SEX IS SIN
exclaims a navy-blue banner sailing through the crowd
with bold white print

To their credit, the men with the banner, who alternately huddle around it like a lodestone and spread through the crowd like feelers, are not reducibly homophobes. Draped from their shoulders, in the spirit of *Corinthians 6*, are full-length body posters decrying fornicators, liars, blasphemers, adulterers, thieves, hypocrites, drunkards, abortionists, witches, atheists, and money lovers. They are in the right place on this Mardi Gras day in New Orleans.

One could enjoy this scene from any of the wrought-iron balconies overlooking Bourbon St. On one such balcony, a petite woman with woven dark hair and stunning violet eyes (no one could forget the eyes), costumed as a fairy queen, surveys the festive crowd below. The unholy throng carouses the street in waves. The fairy queen disappears from the balcony. The crowd revels to a crescendo and subsides.

The fairy queen is again on the balcony but with her back to us. A red chrysanthemum is in one hand. After a moment, she falls, face up, arms spread like an angel in flight as her body nears the street.

7

Chapter 1

A rickety old paneled Datsun mini-wagon clunks into a supermarket parking lot. Phil, nerdy, early thirties, image of mediocrity, gets out. He tries a couple of times to shut the door but the latch works poorly. He finally kicks it shut and heads toward the store.

"Piece of shit," our hero mutters.

Phil browses the cake counter for a second. A hefty, middle-aged woman stands behind the counter.

"I'll take that pink and yellow one. And could you put 'Happy Birthday Mary Elizabeth' on it?"

"Too long," says the countress, heavy, languid, but with a spirit like a coiled spring. Phil wonders. Her hostility. Is it racial animus? Does the black woman behind the counter resent his whiteness? Is she simply beaten down by the drudgery of her job?

Phil wipes his glasses. "What do you mean, too long?"

"It's too long, baby. All them letters on that lil' cake. How about just 'Happy Birthday'?"

No, she is not hostile. Phil remembers what Hermia said. He needs to allow for different personalities. But now he is aggravated.

"I can't take a cake with just 'Happy Birthday'! It won't look ... it won't be special."

"How about a bigger cake?"

Yes, she is hostile.

Phil browses impatiently.

"OK, give me that one."

"Which one, baby?"

9

No, she is not hostile. But Phil cannot tone it down all the way.

"That one there. The one the size of Rembrandt's 'Night Watch.'"

The server pulls the cake from the display case. She is mumbling, shaking her head. "Heard a no cake look like a watch."

Phil fidgets as the server decorates the cake. She brings it over. It says, "Happy Birthday Mary Elizabeth," and has a watch at the center. He looks at it, cocks his head.

"What's that?"

"You said you wanted a watch."

"I didn't say I wanted a watch."

The server sighs, moves her chin slightly, and shouts toward a woman by the oven.

"Hey, Bertha, you heard that man say he wanted a watch?"

"Yeah, sugar. He said a watch."

The server looks back at Phil.

"Bertha heard you say a watch."

Yes, she is hostile. Phil does not need this.

"OK, OK, look, can you just turn it into the star of Bethlehem or a gift from the wise men."

"I thought you said it was a birthday cake."

"Yeah, well, it's Twelfth Night, too."

"Twelfth Night? What the hell is that?"

"Feast of the Epiphany."

She looks at him puzzled, as if awaiting an explanation. There is empathy, connection in her puzzlement.

"Epiphany," Phil repeats. "Today's the feast of the Epiphany."

* * *

An art show is being held in a large, old, city home. People, some in costumes, are viewing paintings and art objects. A black cat masker observes a dark, richly colored landscape. She hears a voice.

"Too dark."

She turns, startled by a close-up red and black Satan mask.

"Darkness," says the Satan masker, "always comes with a tinge of light, doesn't it?"

She moves on, uncomfortable.

* * *

Phil is in the parking lot with a couple of bags and the cake. He tries clumsily to put the cake on the roof of car, but it slowly slides off and crashes face-down in the parking lot. We in the audience well up with tears.

* * *

A burst of laughter at the art show. The Satan masker is away from the laughter, observing another landscape including an apparent pagan ritual. He hears a voice.

"So you prefer something with a little wild energy?"

The Satan masker pauses, then turns to the see the black cat.

"It's in my nature," says Satan.

He gestures to the painting.

"It reminds me of Eden after the fall. Lost in paradise."

The black cat thinks. "But wouldn't you rather more…"

He walks away while she is speaking.

"... brush strokes?"

* * *

The black cat masker is leaving the house, still partially costumed, baby-faced and thirtyish, saying goodbyes. As she leaves, she sees the Satan masker, still fully costumed, struggling to get the dark landscape they had looked at originally into the trunk of his expensive car.

She approaches and speaks.

"You bought it!"

"Yeah, but it doesn't seem to fit."

She steps over to help.

"Haven't you ever packed art before?"

"Not really. "

She gently jostles in the painting.

"You know, you're not the typical art show guy."

"Really?"

"Most of these people actually work bussing tables or selling soap. They come to these things for free wine and cheese, but they can't even afford to buy Christmas cards."

The Satan masker doesn't respond.

She pushes on: "You must be rich."

He flips off the mask to reveal the face of an attractive black man, early thirties. He smiles his best PR smile.

"Gus Grayson, pharmaceutical sales."

12

He holds out his hand. She takes it.

"Hermia."

There is a moment of silence, though we should not imagine it an awkward silence, before she continues.

"Well, you picked the right costume."

"How about a cup of coffee?"

"I have to go to a party."

"Right this minute?"

"With my boyfriend."

"OK, so I won't ask you to marry me."

Hermia smiles.

* * *

A young child's party is in progress in a family home. Leeza, passing forty with first shoots of gray in her dirty blonde hair, tries to keep things in order. This requires much cajolery and many darting movements. The doorbell rings.

Outside, in front of the small Tudor cottage in Old Metairie, stand Phil and Hermia. Phil is speaking.

"Just don't, you know, get too close. They're crazy, Hermia."

"They're your family, Phil!"

"Yeah, but you know, Leeza will have you taking wheatgrass enemas and Magnus, well ..."

Hermia cuts him off: "Magnus is great!"

"He is great," concedes Phil, "but you might end up his disciple. He might start a whole new religion or something. I'm telling you, Hermia ..."

The door opens. Leeza is there, tucking strands of hair back behind her ear.

"You got the cake, right, Phil?"

"Yes, I got the cake. I mean I had the cake. I mean I did have ..."

Leeza begins to panic in earnest. One can see it under the peach cheek skin and the sagging corner of the lips.

"You don't have the cake," she says. She is called away by screaming kids. Phil and Hermia enter.

Leeza's quiet panic is warranted. In the main room, some kids jump and tear at the small colorful flags and balloons hanging in semicircular strings across the ceiling. Others sit glum, awaiting an excuse to wail. A jumper crashes into a sitter. Wailing begins.

The doorbell rings again. Leeza answers it, half in dread, half in relief to momentarily turn her back on the party. A man masked well as the Grim Reaper enters, stands at the threshold, and speaks. He warbles his voice, deep, resonant, theatrical.

"Like a thief in the night..."

Kids look up and fall back.

"He who fears least ..."

The Reaper steps to the center of the main room.

"shall fall ..."

Here, he brandishes the scythe.

"... first!"

Mary Elizabeth had fallen back with the others, but now her five-year-old body springs like a goat and she rushes the Grim Reaper, her wavy blonde hair leaving a weeping willow trail behind her blue party dress.

"Uncle Magnus! Uncle Magnus!"

The Reaper unmasks to reveal Magnus, mid-thirties, handsome and, as all characters inside and outside the story recognize, very charismatic. He drops the grimness and greets her with joy. The attention of the other kids loosens. Leeza tenses and looks around, judging how best to keep chaos at bay.

"Who wants to play "Duck-Duck-Goose?" she calls out in a sweetly muffled version of Edvard Munch's *Scream*.

The party continues. Magnus and Phil are in a corner of the room, tete-a-tete. Phil is speaking in cupped undertones.

"And it splattered all over the cement like a big blue snowball."

Magnus cloaks a smile, pulls out his car keys and hands them to Phil.

"Phil, go to my car, in the back seat, there's a box labeled 'Maggie.' Rip off the label and bring in the box."

"But Magnus …"

Magnus (decisively): "Now!"

Phil goes.

Moments later, Phil is walking through the dew and cricket atmosphere from the car to the door with the box. He peeks in. It's a cake featuring a spider web, spider queen, and text:

Queen Mab
Spinner of Dreams

The door opens and Leeza appears.

"Phil, come help with the presents."

Time passes. Leeza approaches Phil, who is perched on a kitchen chair in a corner.

"Don't worry about it, Phil. Have some egg nog."

"I can't have egg nog. My stomach."

Magnus taps his glass to still the buzz of activity.

"Attention, attention, please! Kids, come up here and listen closely because there's something very mysterious going on, right now, at this very party."

Kids gather at his feet.

"I'm sure you're all wondering where Mary Elizabeth is."

The kids point to Mary Elizabeth and cry out variously: "Here! She's right here!"

"Where?" queries Magnus in disbelief.

Giggles. Hands thrown up and around in the theatrical manner of kids.

"Where?"

"Here. Right. Here."

Magnus extends his hand toward Mary Elizabeth. She comes and sits closest, preparing to hear the story to come.

"No!" says Magnus, sweeping his gaze across the kids so that each child felt fully and exclusively enclosed in the speaker's regard.

"This," he says, shaking his head. "This is not Mary Elizabeth. This is the famous fairy queen, Queen Mab, who arrived not ten minutes ago in her fairy coach."

The kids are in awe. No, not all of them. Let us say that one, a punk kid, resists the speaker's thrall.

"I didn't see any coach," announces the punk kid.

"Of course not," says Magnus, sweetly but with a hidden barb that leaves the punk kid unsure of whether his gambit was bold or foolish. The punk kid hesitates, and Magnus continues.

"Of course not, child. Queen Mab is tiny, no bigger than a butter bean. It's only through magic that she seems such a big girl. Her coach is an empty hazel-nut. Her wagon-spokes made of long spiders' legs. Her whip is a cricket bone, her driver a small, gray-coated gnat."

But one child is out of focus. It is Mary Elizabeth.

"Uncle Magnus, am I really a fairy queen?"

"Absolutely. I haven't the slightest doubt."

The break in focus restores the punk kid's nerve.

"I don't believe it! Prove it!"

"I can't," confesses Magnus. "I can't prove it."

The punk kid is a little taken aback by his own victory, and searches, without consciously knowing it, for a way back in time to retreat from the scene's conundrum. It is at this point that Magnus saves him.

"Uncle Phil can prove it."

All of our young partiers become quiet at this turn in the tale. Uncle Phil looks around, confused. *I can't prove anything*, he is thinking. Magnus goes on.

"The evidence is in that box."

Phil carries the box to the table. All eyes have shifted from him to the box. His relief at this change in focus is excessive.

"If you are not Queen Mab," says Magnus, "then how do you explain this!"

He taps the box and nods to Phil. Phil opens to reveal the Queen Mab cake. Gasps and then clapping. Thus, with an upstart crow and a finger tap the Gordian knot in twain is cleft.

Chapter 2

The tin-roofed enclosure has an earth floor. Our view is close in. We feel the earth at our feet. A ceremony is taking place. We are in a peristyle in an old neighborhood downriver from the French Quarter. Five participants in Mardi Gras costumes form a circle. The fairy queen from the balcony scene is among them. At the center of the circle is a small pot of smoking herbs. Outside the circle, two elaborate altars are adorned with statues of the Madonna and child, small Egyptian bottles, pineapples, cakes, etc. Symbols are drawn on the walls. Holiday tree lights and candles illuminate the peristyle. One woman, acting as priestess, stands and performs a ritual in front of one of the altars.

"Sister, sister, accept this rum, heat of the spirit…"

She pours a few drops of rum from a small Egyptian bottle, then picks up another bottle.

"Accept this water, cool life-giver…"

She pours from the second bottle and picks up a wooden doll with enlarged flat head, a cylinder body of dark mahogany, and two small arms outstretched on the sides. This golem-like creature – or object – had come from the old days, from the rainforests of Ghana or Ivory Coast, as variously told.

"Accept this akua-ma from mother Africa."

She places the akua-ma at the altar and picks up a black crucifix. At the sound of tin rattling in the wind, one of the participants stands and steps outside.

"And this cross of the Christ."

She places the cross at the altar. The participant interested in the tin sound returns to the circle.

"May the four loas and ancestral guides bind us in one spirit: voodoo, Catholic, Druid, and ghost-keeping Lakota, and all other spirit worlds harmonize for our celebration on this coming day."

The priestess takes a third Egyptian bottle and sprinkles it into the pot at the center, which flares slightly. Drums begin to beat. We look out from the circle to take a wider view. A few people, apparently all male, curve around the perimeter with drums and red head scarves.

One by one, the participants dance and lose themselves to the drumbeat. The priestess's back suddenly arches and her body shakes. Then she becomes deathly still and calls out.

"Hold yourselves!"

They stop.

"The city of the dead is come to life and we are its shadows."

She looks at the others as from a distance.

She sinks under the weight of possession. The others swarm around her to prevent her from falling and lay her on a white sheet.

* * *

A dumpy little house, but not unkempt. "Modest" let's call it. The interior living area is non-descript – old sofa, a box television, outdated but still not extraordinary for the late 1990s. By the way, that is the chosen decade for our story. Bill Clinton is president. Grunge and hip-hop and rave parties are getting traction. Cappuccino shops are suddenly on every corner and personal computers in every home. Pagers, or beepers, which a few years ago had been associated, somewhat tongue-in-cheek, with drug dealers eager to promote themselves as ready-at-hand when a fix was needed, have given way to cell phones, which pop culture assigns rather to the suburban soccer moms of the boring bourgeoisie than to those more dangerous and interesting characters peddling pot, heroin, and crystal meth. Most people, though, simply live their lives with no more notice of these trends than a fish notices water. And why not? Just making it through your life is task enough.

Inside the dumpy house, a candle flickers on a rectangular coffee table, the default center of the room. Hermia sits on the old sofa, floral-upholstered and once colorful beneath the palimpsest of wear, with a book. Phil, a little tense as usual, perched on a kitchen chair in the living room, speaks.

"So who is this Gus anyway?"

"He just bought my painting."

"But you don't even know this guy. For God's sake, you said he's a pharmaceutical salesman. You don't become a pharmaceutical salesman without … without … He could be Jack-the-Ripper's long-lost grandson."

"Phil, could you just be a little bit happy that I sold a painting?"

"Yeah, but now he's hanging out at the health food store where Leeza works? It's creepy."

"So he read something about genetically engineered vegetables and went looking for organic produce at the Wheat Seed. He doesn't 'hang out' there. Who put a rat up your ass?"

She gets up to leave the room.

"Wait! You're right, Hermia. I don't know. It's just things just aren't going so well at work."

Hermia pauses, hovers for a moment between potential and kinetic energy, then sits back down on the couch. She picks up a book from the holding shelf underneath the end table.

"Here's the exercise from the Course in Miracles. Let's just try it."

"A Course in Miracles? Isn't that some kind of Christian cult thing?"

Hermia slams the book shut.

"Phil, it's not work where things aren't going well. It's us. And you know it. We're not connected any more. This is not healthy any more."

"Ok, Ok, I'm sorry, let's try."

Hermia opens the book.

"When couples start getting tired of each other, they often fight about nitpicky things, and they think the nitpicky things are the problem, but they're not. The real problem is deeper and something completely different. So the exercise goes like this: We each say, 'I am not upset at the other one for the reason I think I am.' So I'll go first: 'I am not upset at Phil for the reason I think I am.'"

She gestures to Phil. Phil jumps.

"I am not upset at Hermia for the reason I think I am."

"Good. Now we take turns filling in the nitpicky reasons to get them out of the way. I am not upset at Phil because he doesn't appreciate my art."

"I am not upset with Hermia because she pushes me too hard."

"I am not upset at Phil because he won't take a day off work for me."

Phil squirms. His lips tighten. He feels himself escalating.

"I am not upset with Hermia because she sneaks cigarettes on the back porch when she thinks I'm not looking."

Hermia senses hostility, delivers the next line.

"I am not upset at Phil because he's BORING with a capital B."

"I am not upset with Hermia because she lays on the couch all day eating potato chips while I work."

Hermia slams book.

"Forget it."

She gets up and heads to the bedroom. Phil follows.

"No wait! Hermia!"

She slams door before he gets there.

"Hermia!"

Shuffling noises are audible behind the door.

"Hermia, what are you doing?"

"Packing.

"But you're not going to Lafayette to see your sister till Mardi Gras. That's not till next month."

Hermia cracks the door to speak through.

"You're right, Phil. That gives us a month to get this relationship straight. Or I'm not coming back."

She slams the door into Phil's fingers.

"Ouch! Jesus! Maybe you can get Gus to drive you."

* * *

A checkered carpet, black and brown. Cubicles with divider walls, off-white. Lots of light from overhead fluorescents in the drop-ceiling. The cubicle-carved interior workspace of the late twentieth century has arrived.

"This is Finn."

The speaker, a largish man with blond curls, sits in one of the cubicles, wears a business casual shirt, holds the phone with one elbow on the desk.

"All done. I shipped it overnight. If it doesn't meet the spec, call me and I'll take care of it right away."

The speaker pauses, then continues.

"No problem. You know we love working with you guys."

Another pause.

"Ha, ha. All right. See you later."

He hangs up, changes expression, and barks at the phone.

"Asshole."

He sees Phil walking past the cubicle opening.

"Hey, Phil, did you finish that design document?"

"Not yet. I looked at it, but it was longer than I expected."

"Hey, that's what your girlfriend told me last night."

Phil is not amused.

"Ha ha," he mutters in mock-laugher. "I'll have it by lunch."

We follow Phil into a two-person cubicle. He takes one of the two empty seats, as the discussion flows freely over the four-foot cubicle walls.

"Lighten up, Phil," says Finn, a little hurt. "You're going to go to an early grave, man."

A mousy voice, probably that of a software programmer deep in his algorithms, calls out across the ether above the modular cubicle walls.

"Finn, y'all talking about the station design for the cretin crew in Memphis?"

"Yeah, Mike," replies Finn. "It's all laid out, we just need the paperwork. Shakespeare says he'll have it by lunch."

Finn gets up and walks behind Phil at the open side of the cubicle. He punches Phil playfully.

"Good work! I think I'll go celebrate with a bowel movement."

A female employee pipes up.

"Hey, would you guys shut up, before I name all of y'all in a sexual harassment suit."

"Sorry, Jen," says the mousy voice dryly. "But sophomoric humor does not harassment make."

"Well I can still wipe your asses out of the database."

"OK, OK. You win, Jen," Finn concedes. "We'll buy you lunch. And if you're nice to us, you can supersize it."

Jen has had enough: "Go to the bathroom, Finn."

Phil picks up the phone.

* * *

Aaauuuuummmm

A group sits on pads. The room is square with white walls, hardwood floors, bamboo blinds blocking the light on the window side. An instructor is teaching a guided meditation class. This is the Sunspot Wellness Center.

"Now, in."

The dozen or so students inhale.

"And out."

All exhale.

"In."

All inhale.

"And out."

All exhale.

"Now, picture yourself in a boat drifting down a stream. All is peaceful around you. You drift along, hearing the stir of the water, the birds in the trees overhanging the banks."

Students concentrate on the images.

"Breathe in … and out ... Now you're on a small stone bridge that crosses over the stream. You're standing on the bridge looking down at the water. Now you're watching yourself go by in the boat. Seeing yourself go by with unlimited compassion."

The sharp kling-klang of a cell phone rings. Leeza stands up from among the participants and scrambles to get at her phone. The instructor nods gently to tell her it's OK, but she remains frantic and stumbles out of the room.

It is Phil calling from his office.

"Leeza?"

"What is it, Phil?"

"Did you see Gus?"

"What? I don't know."

"Come on. Black guy. He buys only organic produce. He doesn't even believe in health food. He just buys the produce because, I don't know, I think he's up to something."

"Phil, why are you obsessing? So Hermia has a guy friend."

"Yeah, but she thinks I'm boring and he's ... he's…"

The door to the yoga workshop is ajar and we hear a loud rattling of tambourines and primitive instruments.

"Jesus, Leeza, where are you?

"The Wellness Center."

"Oh, great. The Wellness Center. Yoga mats on the floor and a bar down the block so disciples can meditate and then go, go drink shots of tequila?"

"Nobody does that."

"Jason told me he did that just last week. Like it was a big joke."

"That's Jason, Phil."

"Jason's somebody."

"Ok, well look, Phil, are you coming to the store after work?"

"Yeah, about 6."

"OK."

They hang up. Phil's cubicle mate, Jerry, soft-spoken, commiserates as Phil turns back to work.

"Hey, Phil, how's it going?"

"OK."

"Your sister called yesterday."

"Yeah, thanks Jerry, that was her on the phone."

"Everything OK?"

"Yeah, fine."

Jerry is taking a few personal items from his backpack, getting set up for the day.

"You want some dental floss, Phil?" he asks.

"No."

"Altoid?"

"No."

"Rectal cream?"

* * *

At the end of an aisle in the Wheat Seed Health Food Store, Phil and Leeza are talking. A man with fine, straight hair all shaped with pony tail holders into little sprouts that shoot straight up, shops with his back to them.

"What anti-oxidants?" Phil asks Leeza. "I can't put pomegranate juice in my stomach. I feel like I swallowed Mount Etna and now it's erupting."

"The stomach is a metaphor, Phil. Your life is erupting."

"What kind of help is ..."

Another customer glares at Phil. He lowers his voice.

"The stomach is a metaphor? What kind of help is that? I need to work. I need something to keep my stomach right. I got diarrhea. I got no energy."

The sprout-haired shopper overhears despite Phil's

muted tone, and turns. His head has an occasional jerky tic when he speaks, which ruffles the sprouts like a minor earthquake.

"You got toxemia, man. You need a wheatgrass enema."

Leeza greets their new interlocutor. "Hey, Ginger. Phil, you remember Ginger?"

"Yeah, Ginger, from Humboldt County. That still the pot-growing capital?"

"I don't know, man. I haven't been there in ten years. I do know that you don't need pot to get high. You just have to get your chi right."

Phil is distracted.

"Phil," cautions Leeza, "you should listen to Ginger."

Ginger nods at the compliment and goes on.

"Some people think that wheatgrass enemas are a little weird, but I tell you what, man. Get yourself some umeboshi plums. Once you're cleaned out, you can feel your chi. But you gotta concentrate. Then you can move your chi around."

Ginger moves his body in bizarre rhythms to demonstrate. Then his cell phone rings, and he changes character quickly to step away and answer. Leeza continues.

"You need to get healthy, Phil. Quit eating processed foods. Get your body in tune, and everything else is ten times easier to deal with."

Soon, Phil is at the register reading the label on his umeboshi plums. He sees Magnus, dressed in his usual white pullover sweater, putting a poster for a lecture on "Recovering Identity" on the bulletin board near the exit. Other new age posters (iridology, reiki, crystal healing, etc.) clutter the board. Two younger women surround

Magnus like groupies. As Phil steps away from the cashier, Magnus smiles at him and waves with a blend of gravitas and good-natured nonchalance. He addresses the young women.

"Not right now. But I have you on the mailing list."

They begin to leave. Magnus turns to Phil and greets him with quiet cheerfulness.

"Come on. I'll take you home in the 'vette."

"Thanks, Magnus, but my car's here."

"Come on, Phil. Always save something to figure out later."

The streets are wet from rain. Magnus is driving a black corvette with real gusto. Phil occupies the passenger seat.

"So, Magnus, what are you doing driving a 'vette? If you can afford a 'vette, shouldn't you be feeding the poor children in India?"

"I can't afford a 'vette."

"What do you mean, you can't afford a 'vette?"

"I just wanted to drive one. When's Mardi Gras this year?"

"I don't know, Magnus. February 19th? 20th maybe."

"Well, I'll probably squeeze out a couple of payments, and then they'll repo it before Mardi Gras."

"I thought simplicity was the path to enlightenment."

"It is, Phil."

"Well, what's all this?"

Phil lifts his hands in an "all this" gesture, not unlike the gesture of benediction, to emphasize the point.

"This is tantra, Phil. The alternative way. The

28

lion's roar. Simplicity is the gradual, the gentle way, the logical way. Tantra is the absurd way. Gets you there by shock. The exercise of spontaneous, excessive passion."

Magnus downshifts to slide around a wet curve in the road. He turns to Phil and breaks into a childlike smile before continuing.

"But tantra is risky. You could simply fall into attachment to the object of your passion. That's a long fall. A huge setback. Like Adam and Eve all over again. Do not pass Go, do not collect $200."

"You don't look too worried," Phil says dryly.

"No, I'm going to take this baby all the way to India."

"Sure, Magnus. You and 'vette going to leap wide oceans in a single bound?"

Now Magnus pulls over so Phil can get the full rhetorical effect. He no longer smiles.

"Look, Phil. India's not really a place. It's an idea. It's a spiritual yearning. It's always the next incarnation. Or simpler, India is that place between death and the next incarnation. Or simpler still, India is death."

After a moment for this to sink in, Magnus begins to pull back onto the road. An 18-wheeler sits on the horn and Magnus swerves back.

"Be careful, Magnus," Phil says. "I'm not ready to go to India yet."

"I know, little brother. I know you're not ready yet."

Chapter 3

The voodoo ceremony at the peristyle continues. Dawn approaches. The priestess stirs, comes to her knees. The others whisper, spread a tarot deck across the cement in front of her.

We hear whispers: "Who is it?" "What is it?"

The priestess speaks: "Our voices are heard."

She fingers the tarot cards spread out before her, and looks, eyes closed, one-by-one at the others.

"All is well for today's great celebration. The healing light advances on chaos. For all…"

She studies the cards. Something is odd.

"For all but one!"

What at first seemed odd is now traumatic. The priestess gasps, holds her heart. Participants swirl with expressions of concern.

"Are you OK?"

"What is it?

The priestess speaks again.

"Strange and tragic. Tragic, but yet…"

Her voice tapers off.

"Strange."

A moss-clad wood nymph pipes in.

"Something's going to happen to one of us!?"

Then a bare-legged, coin-bejeweled gypsy.

"Is someone going to die?"

The priestess shakes her head in the negative, and keeps shaking as she speaks. She weaves back and forth and supports herself against a third participant, a crook-nosed witch of true Germanic origin.

"Someone … no … but how … Someone here … is … already dead!"

* * *

The walls in the yoga room of the Sunspot Wellness Center are bright with sunlight coming through the window. Phil and Hermia sit in a folding-chair audience, as Magnus lectures in front of a "Recovering Identity" banner.

"... four sheaths of identity: intellectual, emotional, spiritual, physical – each of these four sheaths is like a candle flame, and when the four flames are flickering at different frequencies..."

Magnus lifts his hands, holds one behind the other, and flickers his fingers.

"... your identity is scattered and you can't get a hold of it. You need some practice – jogging, meditation, washing the dishes – that can calm you and bring all the flames back to the same frequency. Then you're centered again."

He holds his hands still, palm-to-palm.

"But relationships seem so difficult. People often say, 'I don't know if this person should be a friend or a lover.'"

He makes eye contact with Phil.

"I don't know if this relationship is healthy for me or unhealthy."

He makes eye contact with Hermia.

"All that anxiety. If you can remove that anxiety, each relationship becomes a beautiful form of yoga. But how do you remove the anxiety? Here's an exercise. Everyone think of a relationship that is giving you some anxiety. Now close your eyes and breathe deeply, slowly."

The audience closes its eyes, shifts its collective identity from listener to practitioner.

31

"Now see yourself speeding through time toward old age."

* * *

A car speeds along a rural highway. The car is a black corvette with two figures inside. The driver we know as Magnus by the white pullover sweater.

* * *

Magnus further directs the yoga group.

"You're aging ten, twenty, thirty years. You're dying. Now you've been dead for five minutes. Look over the life you've just lived. All the struggles, the joys, the transitions. Now view the relationship you've chosen for this exercise. See it from that transcendental perspective. The life you've just completed is a spiritual project. In that spiritual project, what added value did you get from that relationship, that instance of human contact?"

Magnus eyes the crowd and half smiles.

"Now open your eyes. Before we go, I'll tell you the story of a pilgrim who went to India. He grew up in a small town about twenty miles from here, lived most of his life here, was a spiritual seeker like the people in this room. And every seeker designs his or her own path like an obstacle course - there's a touch of hypochondria in every seeker."

Hermia nudges Phil as if to finger him as guilty. Phil jerks away as if stung by a bee.

"As if we're afraid to get there too quickly. Well this particular seeker's obstacle, what really shook his composure, was people who took advantage of other people. It drove him crazy. So he was always fighting on

32

the phone with customer service of every possible company to make sure no one screwed him. Slick talkers always trying to sell you something."

Phil nudges Hermia, gestures with his eyes, and whispers: "Like. Gus."

Magnus's voice continues, mellow and steady.

"Next thing you know, this seeker finds himself in India. And among the throngs, he meets all these guys in saffron robes begging for money or rice. And he's not sure if they're holy men or con men."

A snore is heard. It's Gus, wearing a red scarf in another part of the audience. Hermia thinks it's funny; Phil doesn't.

Magnus registers the scene without breaking rhythm: "There's one person who won't be buying the audio tape."

Chuckles. Someone nudges Gus to wake him up.

"So our seeker figures there are ten con men in saffron robes for every holy man. Drove him crazy. Then one day he dropped a rupee in an old man's bowl and the old man says: 'My son. You're full of anxiety. But what you seek to know doesn't matter. Now take off the chains you've made for yourself.' And then it hit home. The difference between holy men and con men doesn't matter. They're two expressions of the same divine spirit. Two petals ..."

Magnus slowly unfolds the fingers on one hand.

"...unfolding on the same flower."

He raises his hands to the prayer position, bows slightly.

"Namaste."

Gus snores again.

"Or as the gentleman in the red scarf might say, 'Breathe deep and let's get the hell out of here.'"

33

Chuckles as the audience gets up to disperse.

* * *

Pirate's Alley dead ends on one side at the flat white stucco wall of the St. Louis Cathedral, and opens onto St. Peter St. at the other. Wrought-iron balconies hang precariously over the narrow passageway, posing no sense of danger to the French Quarter denizens below -- tourists, starving artists, off-duty strippers, and the like – perhaps because those denizens are high on one of the prodigious varieties of marijuana that come in on the ships from Asia and Latin America, or made lazy by the damp air curling over the river levee and swamping the warren of Vieux Carre streets, or maybe one too deep in cups from the Absinthe Bar at the Cathedral end of the passage.

Somewhere along the alley sits a sidewalk café, tables and chairs wrought-iron like the balconies pressing down from above, tropical plants haphazardly arranged to highlight the old New Orleans atmosphere. Phil and Hermia occupy one of the tables. Phil relaxes near a miniature palm in a blue pot shaped to look like the oversized head of a garden gnome.

"This is the way it should be, Hermia. Cool night in New Orleans. Sipping margaritas."

Hermia looks at Phil wistfully, with a hint of nostalgia.

"You're a good guy, Phil."

A youthful Romanian waiter with a first flush of beard approaches with food.

"Vegetarian nachos," he says, and places the plate on the table.

Hermia eyes the beans and guacamole piled on the chips.

34

"Magnus better hurry."

Phil plucks a chip gingerly from the edge of the plate.

"He said he'd be here after he did the schedule at the Center."

Hermia turns flirty.

"That's not what he told me."

Phil likes the flirty turn.

"Oh, and what did he tell you, Miss Privy?"

Hermia leans in and whispers.

"Magnus told me that he was going to get a shot of tequila with Jason."

Phil pauses, not sure how to take this. Magnus and Gus walk up behind. Magnus tags Phil on the shoulder.

"Hey, little brother."

Phil fidgets while Hermia responds to the arriving dignitaries.

"Hey, Gus! We didn't know you were coming."

Gus extends a hand to Phil.

"Gus Grayson, pharmaceutical sales."

Phil has slid into monotone but is trying to stay in the game.

"Yeah, so I've heard."

Magnus calls to the waiter.

"Two more margaritas."

Hermia flits her attention playfully to Magnus.

"Well, first you're driving a 'vette, then you're a yoga teacher, and now a drunk."

Magnus is nonplussed.

"All streams lead to the ocean."

Phil nods to Magnus and Gus.

"So how do you two know each other?"

"Good question, little brother. Gus came up to apologize for his unorthodox form of applause, and it turns out he knows you guys."

"So naturally you invited him to our dinner."

Phil's irritation has drifted to the surface of the gathering. Gus is not one to let it drift unchallenged.

"Is that a problem?"

"No, no, no. No problem. Even the garden of Eden had its serpent."

"Are you trying to insult me?"

"No, I mean that as a compliment." Phil goes on, passive aggressive but matter-of-fact in tone. "To compare you with Satan is to compare you with the archetypal salesman. I mean, he had to sell them that apple …"

Phil is getting carried away with his own discourse. The others' attention drifts away and he finishes his communiqué noiselessly, a soliloquy in the thick of genial company.

"…And the cost? The cost was they had to give up paradise. They had to give up immortality and paradise for this apple, and the guy actually closes the deal! Every salesman should have a family portrait of Satan on his mantel."

Gus is sipping out of Hermia's frozen margarita.

"Mmm. That's even better than 'on the rocks.'"

She curls her lips. Phil cuts in loudly.

"So, Gus, how are sales these days?

Gus turns to Phil and speaks quietly but intensely.

"I don't want to get in your business but you're about to lose everything."

"Careful Gus," says Magnus. "Prophecy is beyond the scope of the pharmaceutical industry. Maybe we should put that on the seminar list at the Center."

"You know what, Magnus?" says Gus, a little ruffled. "I don't believe in any of that crap. I believe in science and reality, not pie in the sky, made-up bullshit. Sunspot Wellness Center! Place oughta be called the Lunar Landing."

Hermia and Magnus smile. Phil merely aspirates in disgust.

"Science is fine in its scope," Magnus says to Gus cryptically.

"Oh? And what do you think is outside the scope of science, Mr. Genie-come-out-of-your-bottle."

"Science deals only with the world of material fact."

"Well that's the world of reality. Everything else is bullshit."

Gus sits back satisfied and takes a sip. Hermia teases her way in.

"Well, Magnus, what do you believe is out there besides the world of material fact?"

"I believe reality is many layers and the world of material fact is one layer."

This is a bridge too far for Gus.

"C'mon. You don't have a shred of evidence that there's anything other than the material world. The rest is just bullshit to manipulate people."

Phil tries to cut in but his comments are once again delivered in soliloquy as the others do their thing.

"Oh great, now we have a pharmaceutical salesman complaining about bullshit artists trying to manipulate people."

"What are you mumbling about, Phil?" queries Hermia. "Loosen up."

"What? Everybody else can fight but I can't?"

Gus is on Phil now.

"Phil, we're all selling something. You're trying to manipulate people through pouting."

"Well I think Magnus is right," says Hermia decisively.

Magnus lifts his glass.

"A woman of taste and genius."

Gus is in disbelief.

"Hermia, how can you agree with him? You're an artist. You devote your life to what you can see and touch and paint."

Hermia runs her finger around the salty edge of her glass, while Magnus steers the conversation.

"Maybe she's merely using sensory reality as a vehicle to take us somewhere else."

Hermia follows up.

"Hmmm. I like the sound of that."

She licks her finger.

Phil calls out for the waiter. "I need another drink. Who needs a drink?"

Gus nods. Phil signals the waiter for two drinks.

"So, Magnus," continues Hermia. "It must be tough being smarter than everybody else."

Magnus smiles, resists the bait, as Hermia keeps going.

"You know, nobody to learn from."

"I've learned something from everyone at this table tonight."

"No, I don't mean knick-knack learning. I mean really learning."

"Oh, really learning." Magnus acts surprised. "Well, I have somebody for that, too. Y'all know Maggie Leblanc?"

"You've mentioned her a few times," says Phil. "Isn't that the name that was on the cake for Mary Elizabeth? No, her name was on the box. The name on the cake was Queen Mab. I thought she was your new girlfriend."

Magnus replies: "Maggie as given name and girlfriend. Queen Mab as the teacher who can guide me through the transcendental spheres."

"Ooh!" pipes in Hermia. "I didn't know yoga could be so romantic."

"Maggie," says Magnus, "is as far beyond me as I am beyond our hardnosed materialist friend, Gus, here."

Gus is more amused than aggravated at this point.

"Well, excuse me Mr. Love Guru, but where is this wonder woman? Why isn't she here tonight?"

"Maggie doesn't drink."

"Magnus," says Phil. "This is the first time I heard you talk about someone like you need them, and not pouring compassion on them."

"Need makes a poor soil for love and enlightenment," says Magnus.

"You talk like she's a thousand years old," says Phil, looking into Magnus's face for clues.

"Quite the contrary, little bro. She's younger than you."

Magnus nods at Gus.

"Younger than you and from a faraway empire like Gus here."

"A thousand years old and now she's a kid," huffs Gus. "You think she's the Messiah but maybe *you* are the father figure in this fairy tale pipe dream."

"You might be right," Magnus says.

Gus is a little taken aback at the apparent compliment.

"You mean you are the father figure?" he ventures.

"No, I'm not the father figure," replies Magnus. "But it's true that Maggie never knew her father."

Our flock of heroes then sat silent for the space of about four seconds.

"I wish I never knew my dad," says Hermia, running her finger again across the salt. "He was an asshole."

As if in miraculous recognition of the conversation turned pensive, the Romanian waiter approaches with four tequila shots, two silver and two gold. He wriggles his narrow hips between tables. Phil wonders if he is gay. The shots are delivered to our heroes' table, which brings Hermia back to full delight.

"What have we here?"

Magnus perks up to Hermia's buoyant query: "A little unconventional yoga technique. I thought our little quartet was playing out of joint. This is just a little something to realign the spheres. The two silver shots are for Gus and Phil, who have more in common than they think. Smile and drink up, boys."

They hesitate, then drink up.

Magnus continues to Hermia: "And for us, the leftover gold."

They drink.

* * *

In the cubicle ecosystem of Phil's office, he and Jerry type at their workstations. Jerry speaks to Phil confidentially.

"Rumor says layoffs next week."

"Yeah, I heard."

"You think we're safe?"

"They'll need to keep one of us, Jerry."

"Shit, Phil. I really need this job."

Phil's phone rings and he answers.

"Hey, Hermia … When's the art show? … Can't we move everything tonight? … Right now? … I can't, I mean I could but …"

Phil scrunches to the side for privacy and whispers.

"There's going to be layoffs … Layoff, layoffs! … I might be laid off … What do you mean by that, Hermia? …"

He hangs up frustrated. Jerry sympathizes.

"What did she say, Phil?"

"She said I might get laid off but I'll never get laid again as far as she's concerned."

"I'm telling you, Phil. Get some other guy to service her on the side. Problem solved. She'll love you more than ever."

"Great! Now I'm getting relationship advice from a homosexual with 200 boyfriends a year."

"Watch your mouth, baby! That really hurts. I'm not a homosexual. Homo, hetero, bi, I feel sorry for all of y'all. Trying to weave a tapestry with only one thread. I like to think of myself as…"

He searches for the right neologism.

"… omnisexual. Kind of like the Andy Warhol of technical writing."

"Omnisexual? Is that really a thing?"

"Not yet, baby, but it will be."

"Well, excuse me, Mr. Warhol, but there is no other guy."

Finn approaches.

"Hey, Philly, don't listen to this guy. He's got a split pea for a scrotum."

"Fuck off, Finn." says the alleged scrotum-challenged interlocutor. "Your Neanderthal masculinity is so passé."

Finn goes on. "Listen, Phil, did I hear y'all say there's another guy?"

Phil gets up briskly to leave.

"Finn, Jerry, there is NO other guy. Hey, Jerry, take my calls, will ya?"

* * *

All is quiet inside the apartment. We recognize the outdated floral couch. Phil and Hermia's apartment. The couch, coffee table with a few magazines, standing lamp, all dark and quiet, all potential energy, as if awaiting a human presence that may come in a minute, in a million years, or not at all. The front door opens and Phil enters from the sunshine outside.

"Hermia!" he calls. "Hermia? I took off work. Come on, let's get your paintings."

He creeps around looking for signs of Hermia. He enters the kitchen. He moves toward the refrigerator, passing a long counter on the left and a small kitchen table on the right. He turns left to check the faucet, which has been dripping lately, continues to the refrigerator at the long end of the rectangular room. A folded note is on the refrigerator. He takes it and reads two lines of a poem on the front of the paper.

> *Roses are red,*
> *Violets are blue.*

"Jesus!" he says. He opens to reveal the closing lines of the poem:

> *Don't wait up,*
> *Oh, and fuck you!*

Phil crumbles the paper. He feels dazed. He walks back to the living room. He drinks. He loses track of time. It must be very, very late. Music plays. REM. Yes, he put the album on the turntable before he opened the last bottle of cheap merlot. The apartment is dark. Another album is on. Something old. Beatles. Phil, drunk, stares at a wall, then the ceiling, in despair, anger, frustration, self-loathing. He lurches to turn up the volume.

There is a knock at the door. He tries with much trouble to read his watch. Another knock. He staggers toward the door.

"Jesus Christ! Midnight! Where the fuck has she been?"

He knocks over a few things getting to the door. He opens to reveal, not Hermia, but Magnus, disheveled in great contrast to his normal demeanor."

"Magnus?!"

"Yeah, little brother. Let me in."

Magnus pushes his way in and flops on the sofa.

"Magnus, what are you doing? It's midnight."

"Sit down, Phil."

"But, maybe, Jesus, let's have a drink."

"Sit down, Phil. Now."

Phil gets the point and sits.

"Magnus, what's wrong?"

Magnus looks at him for a minute. Then speaks.

"You ever hear of the teleological suspension of ethics?"

"The what?"

"It's Kierkegaard. On rare occasions, you have to do something beyond the scope of human ethics, you need to do something 'evil' to serve a higher, transcendental cause."

43

"What do you mean, evil? What's going on, Magnus? Where's Hermia?"

"Kierkegaard's example is Abraham and Isaac. Abraham agrees to sacrifice his son, Isaac, on God's altar."

"What are you talking about, Magnus? What evil?"

"Was Abraham right, Phil?"

"What?"

"Was Abraham right when he agreed to obey God and kill his innocent son?"

"I don't know."

"Because I'm going to ask you to do something, Phil."

"Me?! Why me? I can't do anything."

"I can't go home, Phil. Maybe never. I need to stay here for a while. People are going to want you to disown me. The ethical thing is to disown me. But I'm asking you to take me in."

"What did you do, Magnus?"

"So do you trust me, little brother?"

"Magnus, what's going on? You're scaring me. Where's Hermia?"

"Hermia's OK, Phil."

Phil is relieved and speaks with a bit more confidence.

"Well whatever it is, I can't do anything. I'm, I'm, look at me. How can I do anything?"

Magnus hesitates another second. Then he takes Phil's shoulders and faces him head-on.

"I killed Maggie Leblanc!"

Chapter 4

Disarray reigns at the voodoo peristyle. "Already dead, already dead."

"What do you mean, already dead?" asks the bejeweled gypsy.

"How can one of us be dead?" adds the mossy wood nymph.

"Four weeks dead," stresses the priestess, desolate.

"The message must be mixed up," crackles the voice of the witch.

"Four weeks dead," repeats the priestess.

The participants hang back in silence. A ripple of cold air passes over. One steps forward and drops a red chrysanthemum at the feet of the priestess.

"Is it me, mambo?"

The priestess shakes her head to indicate "no."

A second steps forward and drops another chrysanthemum. She is shakier than the first.

"Is it me, mambo?"

The priestess shakes her head more violently and arches her back. She is pulling back to the other world.

* * *

Someone begins fumbling in the darkness. A door slams and the light goes on. Hermia has just entered the apartment bedroom where Phil is sleeping.

Phil, burdened by a hangover and mental anguish, looks at the clock. 3:00 a.m. He holds his head with his hands over his eyes. He hears Hermia's voice.

"You want to know where I been?"

Phil's replies from the reptile part of the brain:
"Ohhh."

"Let me rephrase. Do you care where I been?"

Phil is slowly coming around, overwhelmed by whatever dream world he is leaving and overwhelmed by whatever reality he is returning to.

"Yes, I care."

"I went out for a drink with Gus."

"Ohhh."

"So what do you think about that?"

"Ohhh. OK."

"What do you mean, OK?"

Phil begins fumbling about to get himself dressed.

"You want to know what else we did?"

"Nooo."

"What do you mean, no? You don't give a shit and you never have!"

Phil gets his pants halfway on and stumbles out, disheveled.

"Where you going?"

"Got to. Go. To work."

"Work!? It's 3 in the morning!"

"Big contract. Call you later."

Phil stumbles into the living room, trips over something, falls. He finds himself face to face with Magnus, half asleep in the sleeping bag over which Phil has tripped.

Magnus smiles, grotesquely it seems to Phil.

"Hey, little brother."

Phil rushes out as if touched by a serpent.

His day at work transpires in haze. Papers move from his desk. He catches words, phrases: "customer concerns about high-level crosstalk"; "trouble tickets have been issued"; "Thanks, Phil, for the quick turnaround."

46

What did he turn around? Someone eating a raw spinach sandwich. It must be lunch. Chewing. "See you tomorrow, Phil. You look beat. Get some rest." "See you, Finn." Was that his own voice? Is that a patch of clouds moving against a blue background, slowly, slowly, forming patterns and drifting apart? St. Anthony's church? Yes, he left work thirty minutes ago. He is kneeling before the St. Anthony statue in a small chapel near the church entrance. He quietly prays.

Magnus sits on the steps outside the church. Phil comes out from the church and sits beside him. After a while, Phil speaks.

"I don't know how long I can take it, Magnus."

Magnus puts his arm around Phil.

"I know, little brother. You've done good. You've been a big help."

* * *

A door closes. Hermia enters the living room where Phil sits.

"So how long is Magnus going to stay here?"

"I don't know."

"What's wrong with him? I think I saw two guys following him yesterday. He's up to something."

"How can he be up to something? He's Magnus."

"I hate to burst your big-ass bubble, but Magnus is human like the rest of us."

"I know."

Hermia softens.

"Maybe you need to be more human, Phil. Let yourself slip a little. Let things go."

Phil struggles to pay attention under the weight of life's distraction. He repeats her words.

"Let things go."

"You know, it sounds crazy, but if you'd just let things go, you could take more control of your life."

"Take more control."

"We need to talk about things, clear the air around here."

Phil looks up, tries hard to press sounds into words. Pressing, thinking.

* * *

An odd electronic device the size of a small flashlight rests on a wooden barrel. A hand picks it up, deftly secures the wiring, and raises it to the throat. It is the fairy queen at the voodoo ceremony. The priestess recovers composure in the background. The fairy queen clears her throat, approaches the priestess, drops a flower as the others had done, and speaks using the device, an electronic larynx.

"Is it me, mambo?"

"My poor child," the priestess says. "Your spirit is entangled with other spirits in this world." She looks down. "But now you need to get free."

The priestess slips back into a trancelike state. Her speech is more methodical.

"You must find the elephant-man. Find his secret … I see a trial by water."

* * *

On a still black bayou a blue heron sits silently on a cypress knee. The water, though, is most still. Eternally still.

* * *

"Trial by fire," continues the priestess.

* * *

A flash of light hurts the eyes, leaving traces of an exploded black corvette.

* * *

The priestess comes out of the trance and smiles benignly. "Then you rest in peace."

* * *

Phil stands in the dull white bathroom of the corporate office. He looks at himself in the mirror.

"Be calm," he says to himself.

He then works up his face to rehearse a confrontation with Gus at the art show.

"Look, Gus." Phil's jaw is tight, his gaze reflecting sternly back in the mirror. "We need to talk."

He pauses. The jaw relaxes. He takes out comb, combs his hair, lays comb on sink, gets back into character.

"Gus, you don't really know Hermia."

He pauses.

"Gus, we need to talk," he repeats, varying the pitch.

Finn enters in his typical boisterous manner. Phil jumps a foot high, knocks the comb flying, bends to pick it up.

"Hey," booms Finn. "What are you doing? You

were pissing in the sink!"

"What?" Phil is panicking.

"You were pissing in the sink! I saw you!" says Finn, louder than ever.

"No," says Phil, disordered, confused. "No, I wasn't. I swear, Finn."

"I just saw you!" cries Finn. "You were rushing to put your dick back in your pants when I walked in!"

"What?!" Phil is no longer able to form any other words. He holds up his comb as if perhaps it held the secret mark of his redemption. "What?!"

Finn pauses significantly, then bursts.

"Gotcha! Hahahaha!" He pokes Phil's ribs.

Phil is near tears. Finn notices.

"Hey, what's a matter, Phil? I heard you on the phone. Girl problems?"

Phil is helpless.

"Yeah, actually Finn, I think Hermia is seeing another guy. I gotta go talk to him."

"Talk! That's the worst thing you can do. Don't talk, demand! You gotta play tough. Threaten to kill him."

"I haven't been in a fight since third grade."

"That doesn't matter, Phil. You got the guy code on your side."

"The guy code?"

"Yeah, a guy never screws with another guy's woman. And if he does, he knows he's breaking the code. He has to back down when challenged. Your role is to play tough and his role is to back down. Trust me, if the guy's fucking your girlfriend, he knows the code. You won't have to fight."

"So, so what do I say?"

Finn leans close to Phil's face and speaks in a vicious whisper.

"You say, 'Fuck you, you fucking fuck!'"

Finn steps back and smiles.

"You're in old Finn's area of expertise now, my friend."

Finn begins to exit.

"Wait, Finn." Phil is pleading. "Don't tell anybody."

"Of course not, pal. We're friends. Remember: 'Fuck you, you fucking fuck!'"

He exits. Phil enters a stall and sits agonized. He takes out a post-it notepad and writes: "(1) Police (2) Gus."

Jerry is typing at his workstation. Phil enters, stuffing a post-it pad into his back pants pocket. Jerry stops and looks at Phil compassionately.

"Hey, Phil, so Hermia's playing the field after all, eh?"

Phil looks at Jerry in disbelief.

"Let it go, Phil. The guy's doing you a favor."

Finn approaches.

"Hey, Phil," he bellows. "No advice from split-pea scrotum."

"Finn," musters Phil. "I can't believe you, Finn."

"Whaaat?" drawls Finn. "We're all friends. Don't sweat it. So there's another guy."

Jerry pipes in: "And Cotton Mather here can't accept his blessings."

Phil begins to walk out.

"What blessings?" asks Finn, in earnest, his bulging brown eyes turning to Jerry.

But Jerry is already typing. "Go back to your cave, Finn."

* * *

A police station stands at a distance from the street. Phil drives up in his old car and parks on the street in front. He looks in his mirror. He is extremely nervous about the thought of turning Magnus in. He lays his head on the steering wheel to gather his strength. A sudden, vigorous tapping at the window jolts him up.

"Driver's license and proof of insurance," demands the cop.

Phil fumbles to produce the documents.

The officer studies them, calls in on his radio, begins to write on his pad.

"Is everything alright, officer?"

The cop scribbles for a few moments before answering.

"No. Everything's not alright."

The cop steps around the rear to double-check the license plate.

Phil's heart pounds. He no longer knows what is big and what is small. Is this a minor inconvenience or is this the end. The cop returns to the window.

"Your inspection sticker expired two months ago."

He continues writing the ticket.

"I guess you don't think inspection stickers are important."

"Yes, sir," says Phil.

"Yes, sir, you don't think they're important. Or yes, sir, they're important."

"Yes sir, they're important."

The police officer leans in the window.

"Well, if they're so goddam important, why ain't you got one?"

Phil squirms.

52

The police officer mutters as he finishes writing Phil up.

"People like you let your cars go to shit. Next thing you know, you're splattering kids all over school zones."

He passes the ticket to Phil.

"Yes, sir. Thank you."

The cop exits. Phil is falling apart. He looks at the police station for a minute. He takes out his post-it, crosses out (1) Police, (2) Gus, and writes in (1) Gus, (2) Police.

After a moment to quell tears and slow his heartbeat, Phil continues driving through the city. He looks in the rearview mirror to rehearse the confrontation with Gus.

"You know what, Gus?"

He speaks in the role of Gus.

"What, Phil?"

"Fuck you, you fucking fuck!"

Phil stretches his face muscles, turns the mirror toward his face, and tries again in various intonations.

"FUCK you, you fucking fuck ... Fuck YOU, you fucking fuck ... Fuck you, you fucking fuck!"

Horns screech outside the window. Phil has begun to weave. A nearby driver in an outdated muscle car yells.

"Get off the road, asshole."

Phil is shaken and barely mutters under his breath.

"YOU'RE an asshole ... you fucking fuck."

* * *

The interior space seems carved into geometrical primitives: a small square room, a long narrow hall, a large square room, a winding staircase closed off to the

53

public. The walls are red brick but covered with large white panels, and on the white panels, paintings.

People mill around, wine glasses in hand. Gus wanders from painting to painting, aimlessly but stopping to look at each.

Outside the gallery, a row of low hedges guides the walker from the sidewalk toward the door. The walker is Phil. He is nervous. He enters. He hears a woman laugh and a man's voice, jerks his gaze birdlike to the couple, alert to danger. But they are merely a couple, laughing and looking at paintings. He sees Gus coming down a narrow hallway. Gus stops briefly to view a canvas of bright blotches of dripping paint. Phil, in a small square room at the end of the narrow hallway, turns his back, pretends to study a miniature sculpture of a donkey with wings on a makeshift pedestal, until Gus passes. Phil heads through the hallway from which Gus came into the large square room. He steps toward the wine table, thinks better of it as his stomach burns, and turns away. He eyes the forbidden stairway. He sees Gus approaching in the background. He has an uncontrollable urge to ascend the forbidden stairway. He actually puts his foot on the first step. Then a woman with a martini in one hand laughs and leans back into his path, blocking the stairway. He turns to face Gus, but it is not Gus. Someone has come between them. A tall man with black hair slicked into a ponytail so tight that it gave his face a stretched, severe look. It is Mr. Tyler Rex, host of the party.

"You're with Hermia," Rex says inquiringly.

"Yes."

Rex continues to stare at Phil as if he were searching for something. He smiles and hands Phil a business card.

"If you ever need anything," he says, then turns

and disappears into the large square room at the back of the house.

Phil looks at the card:

Tyler Rex, President
Rex Enterprises
Investment, Management, Advisory

He can barely process what was happening. He is sweating. He rubs the card with his thumb, as if it might reveal something he needed.

"Hey Phil."

Phil jolts his head up. It is Gus.

"Gus," he says by way of greeting, but no air comes out.

But he must talk now. He must. But he can't breathe. Why is his breathing so shallow? Why can't he breathe? He speaks, but there is still no air in it.

"Gus, it's about Hermia. She's my girlfriend."

"I know that, Phil, but there's something else…"

"No, Gus, there's nothing else. You have to, you know, go away."

Now Gus is almost amused.

"Or what?"

"Or, you know, I have to … teach you a lesson."

"You want to step outside and settle this right now?"

Gus sets his wine glass down carelessly between two objets d'art. Phil tilts his head slightly, rewriting the script.

"No, no, but, you know, next time, next time that's it. No more mercy."

"I don't think it will matter anyway, Phil."

"I mean it, Gus. What do you mean, it won't

matter? Is it … I mean, the guy code? No, I mean…"
Phil's mouth is dry. He stops.

"The guy code, Phil? What the fuck is the guy code? I mean, look around, what do you see?"

In his confusion, Phil is reduced to a blank slate of innocence. He no longer remembers if he is supposed to be angry, aggressive, conciliatory. He looks vacantly around in response to Gus's question. What does he see?

"Paintings," Phil says.

"And what DON'T you see?" asks Gus.

Phil thinks hard, childlike, searching for the correct answer.

"Good paintings?" he says interrogatively.

Gus becomes animated.

"No, Phil, Hermia's paintings aren't here. She never showed up."

Phil comes back to reality, stunned. Gus continues.

"Where would she go?"

"To her sister's in Lafayette," Phil says.

* * *

Gus sits on front steps of Phil and Hermia's apartment, kicking dirt at a small cactus transplanted from some alien environment far away. Phil pulls up in the brown-paneled Datsun mini-wagon and gets out. He kicks the car door a couple of times to shut it.

"Where you been?" asks Gus.

Phil is defensive.

"What do you mean, where have I been? Nowhere."

"You're an hour and a half late."

Phil pauses with the key in the door.

56

"I had to do something, OK?"

They enter and look around the house. The house is partially emptied. Two keys are on the table.

"Hey Phil, is this Hermia's key?" asks Gus.

"Yeah," says Phil, downtrodden. "And Magnus's."

"Hermia and Magnus??" exclaims Gus in surprise.

"Jesus!" is all Phil says.

They both look at the keys as if they were signs or poisoned darts or something from the code of Nefertiti.

"We have to go find them," Gus blurts out.

"What do you mean, we have to go find them? You go find them. I have my job. I need to think. I can't just drop everything."

Gus is at the door, about to leave.

"Either you drop everything, Phil. Or everything drops you."

* * *

Phil is in his cubicle with Jerry, who is upset and cleaning out his belongings. A pink slip is on Jerry's desk.

"You were right, Phil. I knew one of us was going to get the axe. But look, if you ever quit, give me a heads up. Mr. Davis said he'd take me back if he ever needed anybody."

"Yeah, sure, Jerry. But you'll get a good job. You won't want to do this mind-numbing crap again."

"That's what you say. I'll probably end up back in Chicago at a meat-packing plant scraping shit out of dead cows."

Jerry scrapes out his desk drawer. Phil types for a moment, pauses in thought. The boss, Mr. Davis, walks up.

"Hey, Jerry, come see me before you go. I have something for you."

Jerry nods. Mr. Davis continues.

"Phil, you gonna be alright in here by yourself?"

"I'll be alright."

"Ok, well keep up the good work."

"Thanks."

Mr. Davis begins to walk away. Phil interrupts him.

"Wait, Mr. Davis."

"Yeah, Phil."

Time passes. The small electric heater at Jen's feet hums across the cubicles.

"What is it, Phil?"

Phil looks at Mr. Davis momentarily as if he does not recognize him. Then Phil speaks.

"I quit."

"What?"

"I quit my job. Take Jerry back."

Mr. Davis stands in wonder. Phil is already at the door. He pulls out his cell phone and calls out to Jerry.

"Hey, Jerry, keep my stuff for me."

There is resurgence in Phil's step as he dials a number and speaks into the cell phone.

"Yeah, Gus? This is Phil."

Chapter 5

"Do trees ever grow out of soil around here?"

Phil is driving. He has decided not to answer stupid questions.

"Look, where they go into the water. It's like little skirts ruffled up at the bottom." Gus is amazed.

The old Datsun flies down the long straight road leading back from US 61 to Interstate 10. Both sides of the road are watery swamp, the kind that produces alligator roadkill. Trees eerie with Spanish moss crowd in and over the perpendicular cut waterways.

"It's called a cypress swamp," Phil says dryly.

Gus changes the subject.

"Did you try calling them?"

"Magnus doesn't have a cell phone."

"What do you mean, he doesn't have a cell phone? Everybody has a cell phone."

"No, everybody who's a pharmaceutical salesman has a cell phone. Regular people have regular phones."

"No, I mean everybody. Like that guy, Ginger, at the health food store."

"How do you know Ginger?"

"Damn, Phil, don't be so uptight. I just wanted to know if Magnus had a cell phone."

"Well, no, Magnus couldn't 'be here fucking now' with a cell phone."

"How about Hermia?"

"She's too broke for a cell phone."

They cruise, silent, onto I-10 West.

Phil adjusts his buttocks and fidgets in aggravation.

"I still don't know why we couldn't take your

Lexus, Gus."

"I told you, it's a company car."

"What's with the scruples? It's a pharmaceutical company. They turn you into a deadened, exploited, alienated slave, and then tell you don't take the car."

"I'm not a slave."

"I didn't mean it like that."

"You calling me a slave. But you mean it in a nice way."

"No, I mean you're in a system that sucks out all your blood and then spits you out. You don't have to help them do it."

"I'm helping them do it?!"

"I mean it's like you're so grateful you won't even put three days wear and tear on their car."

"So now I'm an Uncle Tom. But I'm sure you mean that in a nice way."

"No, I mean yes. I mean, Uncle Tom was a great character in a great book who's been totally misrepresented in pop culture."

"Oh, and I guess your friends in their white hoods been misrepresented too."

"Gus, how can you say that? I'm totally for racial equality. I have Martin Luther King's 'I Have a Dream' speech bookmarked on my computer. I'm a Democrat."

"Maybe I ain't a Democrat."

"What do you mean? You have to be."

"A black man has to be a Democrat?"

"Republican! For Christ' sake, Gus, tell me you're not a Republican!"

"Why not? Give me my tax money back and get out of my way. Then I'll become self-reliant. Then I'll become independent."

"What do you mean, self-reliant? It's the party of

rich white guys. It's the party where the noblest form of human activity they can imagine is piling up more profits."

"What's wrong with making money? That pharmaceutical company you're trying to save my soul from pays me a lot more than whoever pays you to drive this crappy Datsun wagon."

Phil eyes a gas station at the next ramp which boasts of two alligators and a snake farm on the property.

"So, Gus. You really think that making money is the noblest form of human activity? The one measure of the quality of life?"

"What else you got?"

Phil aspirates in disgust. "Figures," he mutters to himself. "I gotta cross two hundred miles of bayou country with a Republican."

"I'm hungry," Gus says. "You hungry?"

"No. look, Lafayette's twenty minutes away. Hermia's sister, Laura, works in a restaurant there. Can you just stifle your, your voracity?"

They cruise. Phil grips the wheel. Gus rolls down the window and lets the air lap in. Phil steers off the interstate and the car passes rows of wood frame houses, pecan trees and screened-in porches as it enters downtown Lafayette.

* * *

Ceiling fans and bayou scenes dot the interior of this fine local restaurant. Cypress trees sprout from the floor and reach to the ceiling. Tablecloths feature crawfish and snapping turtles. The décor is emphatically local for one reason: to bring in the tourists. But the food is no joke. A Cajun band warms up with a fiddle and a washboard.

Locals chatter away in pidgin French. Travelers lured in from the long road between California and Florida, speak in proper English, southern redneck, or Texas twang, as the case may be. Two patrons in particular catch our interest as they look at a menu. These are Phil and Gus.

"What is this shit?" Gus asks. "Bow-den"?

"You never heard of boudin?" needles Phil, pronouncing it *boo-dan* in the lingo of the region.

"Hell no," says Gus. "My people's from New York."

Gus checks out the band, the waitress across the room.

"How can you take this so lightly, Gus? You were more eager to go on this trip than I was."

Gus is reading the menu again.

"Crawfish pie. I know crawfish pie. Get that at Audubon Park."

The waitress approaches the table. She steps up the pace when she sees Phil.

"Hey Phil! How you been?"

"Hey Laura."

Laura turns to Gus, but talks to Phil.

"Who's your friend, Phil?"

Gus answers for himself. "Gus Grayson."

Laura tosses back her dark brown hair and takes his hand flirtatiously.

"Hi Gus Grayson. I'm Laura."

"I heard a lot about you, Laura."

Phil looks on in disbelief and Gus and Laura parley.

"Good, I hope," she says.

"Good as gold." Thus Gus, smiling broadly now.

62

Phil cuts in.

"Laura, you seen Hermia?"

"Yeah, she was here." She turns back to Gus.

"So what do you want, Gus Grayson," she drawls. "To eat, that is."

Gus pretends to look at the menu.

"I'll have some bowden."

Laura laughs and corrects his pronunciation. "That's boo-dan, silly."

"Come on, Laura," Phil interjects. "Where's Hermia?"

"I don't know."

"What do you mean, you don't know? You're her sister."

"She came and left in a whirlwind with some guy said he was your brother ... what was his name?"

"Judas Iscariot," grumbles Phil.

"No," says Laura, "It was ..."

Gus consummates the sentence: "... Magnus."

"Yeah," smiles Laura. "Magnus."

Now she turns back to Phil.

"Phil, what you so upset about? Your back bothering you again?"

"Yeah," says Phil. "I'm still trying to get the knife out that Hermia and Magnus jammed in there."

"Aw, Phil. They said nothing but nice about you. You brother said your life was about to turn for the better."

"Oh, is that how he put it?"

"Yeah, that's how he put it. Now what you want?"

"Just coffee."

She steps away.

"Phil, look at that guy playing the fiddle. You think all he cares about is money?" muses Gus. Phil doesn't quite follow.

* * *

In another time and place, Magnus and Hermia fly along the highway in the corvette.

* * *

"Wake up, Phil," says Gus. He pokes Phil across the table. "Hermia's sister here, Phil, you think she's being nice to us for the money?"
"No."

* * *

Magnus and Hermia fly along the highway in the corvette.

* * *

"Well don't be so down on your culture, Phil. There's a lot of things happening out there."
Phil stares at Gus, trying to figure out the curves of his personality.

* * *

The fairy queen emerges at dawn from the alley of a creole cottage in the French Quarter of New Orleans. Drumbeats indicate that the peristyle is behind the cottage. She wanders down the street through the French Quarter. A few partiers are still out from Lundi Gras night and a few are gathering already for Mardi Gras day. She pauses

64

in front of a two-story cottage on Bourbon Street with pink painted wood siding and forest green shutters enclosing the doors. She takes out a key and enters.

The high ceilings, droopy slow ceiling fans, and dark wood walls indicate age, a place with history. Every cottage on Bourbon Street has a history. The fairy queen sits at a table with a vase of red chrysanthemums and an open envelope. After a moment, she slides out the letter to reread what she has apparently read before. We catch enough glimpses to put it together: "idiopathic lesions on the soft palate and throat ... very destructive ... treatment unsuccessful ... patient requests termination of treatment ... expect rapid decline ... " After a moment, she gets up and pours some water into the vase of flowers.

* * *

Gus plays with a Tabasco bottle. *Try it on soups, eggs, sauces, and gravies.*

Phil takes out the card Tyler Rex gave him.

> *Tyler Rex, President*
> *Rex Enterprises*
> *Investment, Management, Advisory*

He recalls what Rex said: *"If you ever need anything."*

"What about you, Gus Grayson, pharmaceutical sales?" muses Phil. "Is money the measure of your life?"

"No."

"What else you got, then?"

Phil puts the card back into his wallet. Gus places the Tabasco bottle back by the salt and pepper shakers.

"I don't know yet."

Laura serves them.

"You boys gonna stay the night?"

"I don't know," says Phil.

"Yeah," says Gus. "We're definitely gonna stay the night." He says it with emphasis on the first syllable of "definitely."

Phil looks at Gus incredulously. Laura smiles her lazy sprawling smile.

"I get off in an hour. We'll go to Pirogue's for drinks and then y'all come stay at the house."

* * *

Dark brown wood graces the smooth curve of the bar and the solid frame on the mirror of the backbar. A few nets and ship wheels hang from the ceiling. The cash register is circled by a small string of Christmas lights. A neon football helmet shines proudly if incongruously among the high-hung fish nets.

Then the CRACK of someone breaking at the pool table.

"Hey Laura, who's your coon-ass friend?" asks the breaker, a 50-ish man with the markings of hard work, probably in the offshore oilfields. His accent is hard Cajun.

Laura and Gus and Phil sit near the pool table. Gus perks up at the query, but Laura answers before he can react.

"This here, Papa Bear? This is Phil, Hermia's ex-boyfriend. And this is Gus."

Phil is aggravated at the "ex-boyfriend" tag and Gus is a little confused to find that he is not the "coon-ass."

"Hey Gus," calls Papa Bear. "What say you be my

66

partner, cher, and we whip ass on Laura and de coon-ass?"

Laura and Phil and Gus get up to join the game.

"He ain't a coon-ass, Papa Bear. Phil went to college here, but he's from New Orleans."

"Ohhh, das good. Me and Gus waise no time whipping ass on a city boy, ha ha."

They play. Someone calls out from a leather-capped saddle bar stool.

"Hey Phil!"

The speaker hops from the stool and approaches with a longneck bottle of beer in each hand.

Phil spies the approaching patron closely.

"Jimmy?"

"Yeah, Phil, what you think? Yeah, it's Jimmy. Last time I saw you it was in Dr. Sanderson's Sociology class. Somebody brought a pitcher of screwdrivers for the last day."

Phil laughs. "Yeah."

"Well, good seeing you. I gotta get my girl her beer or she'll kick my ass."

He begins to walk off. Then pauses.

"Oh, Hermia said y'all split up. I'm sorry, man, but she said it was friendly on both sides. I always liked that about y'all."

Phil is stunned.

"Hermia?"

"Yeah, she was in here last night with some guy. They left with Diane. Remember Diane from Abbeville? Cursed like a sailor but cute as a button."

Jimmy walks off.

Phil speaks sotto voce. "Yeah, I remember Diane."

He drifts back to the pool table. Papa Bear is

going for the 8-ball.

"And dat ..." declares Papa Bear.

He pockets the eight.

"... is dat!"

* * *

Phil pours himself a glass of Scotch on the rocks. He plops in a floppy chair in Laura's living room. The tiny Christmas lights that hang around the wood frames of her windows look just like the ones at Pirogue's. Laura is rolling a joint. She lights up.

"You want some, Phil?"

"No."

"You don't smoke any more?"

"No. It gives me anxiety."

Laura passes the joint to Gus and walks over to turn up the music. Led Zeppelin IV, it must be.

"Gus," says Phil. "We gotta go to Abbeville."

Gus takes a hit of the joint.

"Sure, man, if you think that's the right thing to do."

"Don't you think it's the right thing?"

Laura returns, takes a hit, speaks before she exhales.

"So you sell shit?"

"Yeah," says Gus. "I sell shit."

He takes a hit, passes to Laura, she takes a hit and speaks again before she exhales.

"What kind of shit?"

They giggle. Laura continues.

"So how'd you two get together?"

Phil interjects from the background.

"We're not together."

68

Gus turns to Laura confidentially.

"He likes me."

They giggle.

Laura ponders.

"Y'all a good pair actually. Phil holds everything inside and you let it all out."

"I don't hold everything inside," contends Phil.

She raises her voice.

"Well why you need them plums you said you been carrying around?"

Louder laughter from Laura and Gus. Gus twists the thought around.

"Or how about you and Phil," he says to Laura. "Introvert and extrovert."

"You calling me an extrovert?" protests Laura in mock-challenge.

This too is funny. Laura pushes Gus playfully, then takes a hit and speaks seriously.

"Wait!" She pauses, alert to some invisible stimulus. "Did you fart?"

Laura and Gus laugh. Laura calls out louder.

"Did you fart, Phil?"

She and Gus laugh hysterically. Then quiet. Gus speaks.

"Did you ever try to fart with a torn stomach muscle?"

Chuckles, then silence. Laura speaks.

"You know what you said about introvert and extrovert? You think somebody could live their whole life thinking they're an extrovert when really they're an introvert?"

"How could they think they're an extrovert and not be an extrovert?"

"I don't know. Like they just looked at it wrong.

You ever see a movie and you think the whole movie's about one thing but it's not, it's really about something else?"

"Like what?"

"I don't know. I can't think of a movie."

They giggle. Laura thinks.

"OK, OK, here's a book. *The Trial* by Kafka."

"Never heard of it."

"The main character is arrested in the first sentence and I kept waiting the whole book to see what he was arrested for, but that's not what it was about at all."

"I don't get it. Sounds weird."

"Like real life," she says.

Gus is losing the thread.

"What?"

"Well," Laura continues. "What if you spend your whole life focused on one thing, like that's what it's about, and it turns out that your life wasn't about that at all; it was about something else."

"Like introvert and extrovert?"

"No, not like that."

She carefully places the roach from the joint in the ashtray and turns intimately to Gus.

"What if introvert and extrovert are not two kinds of people but two aspects in all of us? And our whole lives are defined by this push pull, inward, outward, in, out …"

Gus is getting in the thread now.

"And the same with the whole universe out there. Centripetal and centrifugal. Like breathing in and out. The whole history of the universe is just the history of things getting closer and things getting farther away, things getting closer..."

He scoots up next to Laura.

"... and things getting farther away."

* * *

Magnus and Hermia fly along the highway in the corvette.

* * *

"Things getting closer ..."

Gus and Laura tease a little and get up to go to the bedroom. Phil snores on his floppy chair with his scotch still in hand.

* * *

A two-lane highway stretches and winds between firm land and swamp country. The Datsun wagon is plugging along. Gus speaks while fiddling with the radio dial.

"I don't know why you care so much where Hermia and Magnus are going."

Phil's reply shows little emotion.

"Who cares. And you were going to be her boyfriend. What a catch."

"I wasn't going to be her boyfriend. Look, if someone doesn't want to be with you, then why would you want to keep the relationship going? I could never understand that. If somebody wants to leave, why would you get mad at them for leaving. It seems more logical to get mad at them for staying. I'm a realist."

As a preface to his reply, Phil reaches out of the driver window to swat at the ebb and flow of swamp

71

insects.

"You're not a realist. A realist knows that you need commitments and, and arrangements, you need to make deals and stick to them even if they're not always pleasant."

"OK, man, you win. I'm an idealist. I'm in it for the love. And when the love is over, part friends and move on."

Phil rolls his window back up. Then back down.

"Like Laura?" he asks in a tone of rhetorical questioning.

"Yeah," Gus says. "Like Laura."

Chapter 6

Another Cajun diner. They all start looking the same. The dark rustic wood. A splash of neon signs. Bustle of chairs and clinking glass and Cajun accents over a card game of Bourré. A sense of oasis against the dark heavy night outside.

This particular diner is in Abbeville, a true Cajun town, compared to which Lafayette seems a metropolis. Phil and Gus sit at a table. Phil is on the phone.

"Yeah, Peter? Hey it's Phil ... Well, look, I'm in Abbeville. I'm trying to find Diane. Do you have her number? ... Well do you know where she lives? ... What do you mean she left town? I saw Jimmy last night and he said ... What do you mean Jimmy's an asshole? He can't be an asshole, he, he ... Yeah, yeah, OK, Peter, thanks."

He hangs up.

"What did he say?" ask Gus.

"We can stay at his house tonight. No one's going to be there."

* * *

The sound of crickets drones up and down. In front of a wood frame house on the outskirts of town, a statue of a porcelain Negro in uniform stands tilted in the soft earth between the paved walkway and the hedges that spread across the front of the house.

A hand tilts the statue still further, reaches under it, and pulls out a key.

"Nice guy, your friend, Peter," says Gus. "I always wanted to stay in a house with a porcelain Negro in the yard."

"It's just a statue," Phil says. "Probably a relic of somebody's great grandpa."

They go in. It is a non-descript bachelor pad with an empty pizza box on the coffee table and muddy work boots in the corner. Soon Phil and Gus are dozing off in sleeping bags on the floor.

Phil wakes to noises outside. He creeps to the door, opens gently, steps out. Something is moving on the side of the house. Phil picks up the porcelain Negro and holds it clumsily in both hands as a weapon. He creeps to the corner of the house, peeks around, turns the corner. He cannot see for darkness. His heart leaps as he crashes into Peter, goggle-eyed and drunk.

"Shit! Peter!"

"Hey, man. I had to come home. Monica kicked me out."

"Sure, it's OK, it's your house."

They go in and stand in the living room.

"Locked out of my own house. Ain't that some

shit."

"Yeah, yeah, it's, uh, some shit."

Peter notices Gus asleep and says now in a tone of astonishment.

"Ain't that some shit?!"

Phil, confused: "Yeah, it's, uh, really some shit."

"Let's go into the kitchen," says Peter. "I need a coffee. You need a coffee?"

Peter rummages around to get water boiling.

"No thanks, Peter. I can't have caffeine this late."

Gus, in his sleeping bag, hears a loud bang and cursing as the drunken Peter spills the hot water. Gus sits straight up.

In the kitchen, Peter is agitated from the burn and the mess.

"You alright?" Phil asks Peter.

"I'm alright. Yeah, you alright?"

"Am I alright? What do you mean, am I alright?"

Peter lowers voice.

"Phil, you didn't tell me he was a nigger."

"I didn't think of it."

"You didn't think of it! You can't tell by looking at him?"

"I guess I wasn't looking at him that way."

Gus stands behind them, unnoticed, in the doorway, as Peter continues.

"Wasn't looking at him that way?! How many ways can you look at him?"

Peter and Phil are stunned to see Gus in the kitchen doorway.

* * *

Gus and Phil, laden with their sleeping bags, head

from Peter's door to the Datsun in the driveway. Phil stubs his toe on the porcelain Negro, puts down his bag, and with groan and effort pushes the statue over into the low hedges. Peter comes up behind them and stands in the doorway as they drag their way to the Datsun.

"Shit, man," says Peter ruefully. "I didn't mean it like that. I got nothing against black people. But my neighbors, man. I gotta live with these people."

Phil turns as he opens the car door.

"Peter?"

"Yeah?"

Phil finally delivers the next line like he owns it.

"Fuck you, you fucking fuck!"

They drive off, hurtling into the darkness of the Louisiana two-lane highways. Eventually, the old Datsun putters into one of the rare rest areas at the side of the road.

They both fall asleep in the front seat. Phil wakes to find Gus in the crook of his shoulder, sleeping against his chest. Phil is paralyzed in confusion for a second, then relaxes and falls back to sleep with Gus still against him. He dreams of his childhood. Leeza was reading a book. *Grimms' Fairy Tales*. "Little Red Riding Hood." In the picture, the wolf blocked the girl's path. And other stories. "Sleeping Beauty." Something about "Sleeping Beauty" terrified Phil. All he remembered was wanting Magnus there.

The sun through the car window wakes Phil up. He looks around and doesn't see Gus. He gets out of the car and stands confused, anxious. Then he hears Gus's voice.

"Hey Phil, come see this!"

Phil sees Gus peek out from the edge of the woods. Phil joins him. Gus is looking into a creek.

75

"Look," he says to Phil. "These crawfish look like ghosts."

"Ghosts of their former selves," says Phil.

"What?"

"They're molting."

"Crawfish molt?"

"It's the only way they can grow. Throw off the old shell that's getting too tight."

"Kind of like people," says Gus.

Phil smiles at the observation.

"Yeah," he says. "Kind of like people."

* * *

At on old gas station with a JAX BEER sign, Phil is pumping gas. He sees a black corvette driving out of the parking lot. He uncharacteristically leaps into action and chases after the corvette, catches it, bangs on the window, and yells.

"You fucking fuck!"

Someone gets out of the corvette, but it is not Magnus. The stranger gets rough and knocks Phil down. Gus runs over and intervenes. The fight stops. The roughneck gets into the corvette.

"… you and your pet nigger," he grumbles.

The corvette pulls off.

"You OK?" asks Gus.

"Yeah, he broke my glasses."

Phil limps back to the Datsun with Gus's support. They continue down the country road. All seems fine, but then a siren sounds. Phil pulls over and the cop approaches the car and taps the driver window. Phil rolls it down.

"Heard you boys had a little trouble."

"What do you mean, officer? Is everything alright?"

"I don't know if everything's alright. Y'all look like y'all from out of town."

"Just New Orleans," Phil says.

"Two boys from New Orleans starting a fight at the convenience store ain't exactly what I'd call everything alright. I'm going to have to run a check on you."

"That guy in the corvette? He tried to kill me! That guy was an idiot." Phil is worked up.

"Get out of the car," says the cop.

"I didn't even …" starts Phil.

"Get out of the car."

Phil gets out.

"Spread'm."

The cop starts to search Phil.

"You shouldn't oughta called my nephew an idiot."

"Your nephew?"

"Yeah, he told me everything happened. How you attacked him."

"I attacked him?!"

"You saying you didn't?"

"Of course, I didn't. The guy would have ripped my face off."

"I tell you the truth, I don't trust the little bastard myself. But lil' Naquin's my nephew. And blood's thicker than water. Everybody gotta take care of their own. I bet you take care of your own when you back in New Orleans, don't you?"

"Yes sir," says Phil in resignation. "Of course, I do."

"Well there you have it. I'm not gonna run you in for assault."

"Thank you, sir."

"I'll just book you with disturbing the peace. Get your friend there to bring $100 to the courthouse after lunch and we'll let you boys go home."

Phil whines as the cop puts him into the squad car.

"I can't go to jail. I'm, I'm, I have a respiratory condition. I'll be sodomized."

The cop slams the door and turns to Gus.

"Mister, I heard what happened. What my nephew said. Boy ain't got no manners. I oughta let you whip his ass."

He gets into the car and then turns back to Gus.

"Next time you just whip his ass and I'll look d'other way."

The squad car drives off with Phil in the back seat. Gus pulls money from his wallet, peels back bills: 20-40-60-61.

* * *

The Datsun pulls up at a country store with a Western Union sticker in the window. Gus gets out of the car, kicks the door twice to close it, and pulls open the screen door of the run-down building. Inside are two old Cajuns, Thibodeaux and Arceneaux. One of them, or perhaps a relative, must have a taxidermy hobby, as the primary décor on the walls consists of formerly living raccoons, owls, bobcats, and a few swamp creatures Gus has never seen. Arceneaux, the older, who never seems to move from his rocking chair, speaks first.

"Hey, Thibodeaux, help dat fella."

"I'm stocking dem Coke, Arceneaux, you help da fella."

"I'm ressing my dogs, Thibodeaux. You get ole as

78

me, you'll see."

Thibodeaux stops stocking and goes to help Gus.

"I had $300 wired from New York," says Gus.

"Ooo-wee. $300 enough to buy dis ville morte."

Thibodeaux's bon mot awakens Arceneaux.

"Don't make fun o' my town, Thibodeaux. I'll send yo' ass back to Breaux Bridge."

"At least Breaux Bridge got dat Jake Delhomme, NFL quarterback."

"Jake Delhomme ain't in Breaux Bridge now, is he?"

Thibodeaux turns to Gus.

"You heard o' Jake Delhomme?"

"Sure," says Gus. "New quarterback for the New Orleans Saints."

"See now, Arceneaux. Dis boy know all about Jake Delhomme"

Arceneaux takes an interest. He finally stands and comes to look closely at Gus.

"You wit dat city fella in dat fight with lil' Naquin?"

Gus is steely silent, not sure what to expect. Arceneaux continues.

"How y'all did dat fight?"

"My friend saw his corvette and thought it was somebody else."

Arceneaux and Thibodeaux burst into laughter, but Gus is out of his element and unsure if the laughter is friendly or malicious. Arceneaux's next line puts his uncertainty to rest.

"Wish y'all a killed that lil' bastard, Naquin. Nothing but trouble."

Arceneaux goes back to his chair. He and Thibodeaux watch Gus back out on the gravel.

Thibodeaux shakes his head.

"Dem boys in for troubles and trials eh, Arceneaux? What you tink?"

Arceneaux has lost all interest and is back in his own world.

"Je'n c'est pas."

* * *

Phil sits in the lone cell of the parish prison. He stares at the wall, then the ceiling, then the wall again. He takes out the card from Rex. *If you ever need anything.* He finds a blemish here or there as a focal point, shakes it off, picks up the cell's one accoutrement, a Bible, and browses. He begins to doze. The cell door bangs and Phil jumps. Gus bails him out.

Phil takes the passenger seat in a daze. He has lost sense of time. Gus is driving. It is night. The Datsun limps along a two-lane road. No rest area appears this time. Gus is tired. They stop and switch drivers, but Phil cannot drive. Not yet. The car turns and goes a little ways down a narrow road and pulls off to the side. Gus and Phil fall into a dreamless sleep.

Chapter 7

TAP ... TAP ... POP-POP-POP. Whoa! Shit!

Phil leaps up, popping the ash tray, jerking the steering wheel, and startling Gus.

The rapid staccato banging on the driver's window begins again. Phil squints in the darkness. Inches away from his face, separated by a thin sheet of glass, is the face of a quite possibly insane black woman, fiftyish. Phil is confused, reaches for his wallet, his keys, cracks the window. The woman stares directly at him. There is no nonsense in her look.

"Get up, ya fool!" she yells. "Cops coming!"

Phil and Gus try to perk up. A cop pulls up with lights flashing, gets out and walks up. Phil's life seems peopled by cops lately. He wonders if this symbolizes something. Then the sound of the cop's voice refocuses his attention. The cop tips the bill of his hat to the black woman.

"Ma'am Peychaud. Watcha say?"

"Fine evening, JC," says Madame Peychaud.

"For what, I don't know," says the cop.

"Starry night," says Madame Peychaud. She stretches out her hands and wiggles her fingers. "Lots of vibration from the sky."

"You know your business and I know mine," says the cop. "Who's in that car?"

"Old friends. Got lost trying to find my house."

The cop sticks a flashlight in the window. Phil is fumbling for insurance papers. Gus is beginning to snore again.

The cop steps back and resumes the conversation with Madame Peychaud.

"Damn shame they ever built that interstate. People treat the back roads nowadays like another planet."

"Be careful what you say about the planets, JC. They listening. Sure as you standing there, they listening."

The cop is returning to the police car.

"Maybe you right, Ma'am Peychaud. Don't let the alligators eat them idiot friends of yours."

He drives off. Madame Peychaud wheels on Phil and Gus, deadly serious again.

"What the hell's a matter with you. Parking wherever you damn please. You lucky you ain't in jail or shot for ducks."

Phil stutters.

"We, we, I was too tired to drive."

"You think you can drive a couple a miles up the road?" she asks sarcastically.

"Yeah, sure," says Phil, childlike, putty in her hands.

"Well come on then."

She gets in her decrepit old pickup and leads them down the dark, swamp road. After what seems much more than a couple of miles to Phil, they turn left onto a narrow dirt road with trees hanging overhead. The moonlight glistens in the moist, dense air. Then another left and they are back on a two-lane road. The moon has disappeared into the foliage. With each turn now, the night seems darker. In the distance is a picturesque old shack. Closer and closer it gets. The old pickup eases toward the shack. There is a sign in front:

MADAME PEYCHAUD
PSYCHIC WONDER OF THE WORLD
Palmistry, Tarot, Planetary Healing,
Guardian Angel Consultations

As they pull up, the muffler is dragging on Phil's car, which has slowly been deteriorating. They get out and walk to the steps. Phil notices moss growing in the cracks of the steps, living crawling pipe cleaners of verdant green.

"Um, excuse me miss – madame – Peychaud. Do you know us?"

Madame Peychaud slaps the sign.

"See that sign? Of course, I know you."

She swings open the screen door and they enter.

"Now y'all get some sleep," she says. "We'll talk in the morning."

Phil and Gus stretch out on the wood floors with their bedrolls as Madame Peychaud heads for the back of the house. They begin to doze. The shack is perfect for weird dreams – set deep enough in the swamps to fill with the sounds of crickets, frogs, and swamp birds, a kitchen filled with small Egyptian bottles not unlike the ones used in the voodoo ceremony.

* * *

In a timeline awaiting our heroes' pass, a deft-fingered hand pours from one Egyptian bottle and then another into the steaming water in a sink. The head goes face down with a towel over the back to give an aromatic steam bath to the face and throat. The head comes up. The mirror shows for the first time the natural face of the fairy queen in the Bourbon Street cottage. Cracks are beginning to appear prematurely in the skin at the corner of her exquisite eyes. She applies two fingers to her throat where the electronic larynx was used. She speaks softly to test her voice.

"Is it me?"

She smiles a small Mona Lisa smile.

In Madame Peychaud's shack, Phil and Gus stir half awake. Madame Peychaud throws open the door.

"Come on get some coffee y'all."

Phil and Gus look at each other in partial confusion, then get up and head toward the back of the house.

In the kitchen, a fantastic scene of stone and clay and cast iron, Madame Peychaud is serving coffee. Phil and Gus are nervous, searching for something to say. Phil takes a plunge.

"So, uh, how's the uh psychic business these days?"

Gus cringes at Phil's opening gambit.

"Bad," says Madame Peychaud abruptly. "Since the interstate come, there's no more traffic on this road. No rambling man looking for the next pot of gold. No bored housewives looking the see who's cheating with who. No nothing. So I'm stuck here like a spider waiting for a fly."

Phil and Gus sit, waiting for someone to make the next move. Madame Peychaud does so.

"Just like in that movie, *Psycho*. Ha, ha, ha."

This piece of intelligence does little to comfort Gus and Phil. Phil clams up. Gus now tests the waters.

"You don't really know us, do you?"

Madame Peychaud turns serious.

"Not the way you mean. But I know you all the same. You come here cause y'all seeking something. He (gesturing to Phil) almost knows it. You (gesturing to Gus) don't know it yet. But that's why y'all here."

All sit mum. Phil and Gus are trying to figure out how to proceed. Madame's Peychaud's raspy voice breaks the silence again.

"Ha, ha, ha." She shakes her head.

"What's so funny?" queries Gus.

"I'm thinking of the other reason y'all here."

Phil, torn between awe and curiosity, pipes back in.

"The other reason?"

"Yeah, y'all come on out back and I'll show you."

They exit back door. The back porch sits on a yard that tapers down to the bayou, where there is a broken-down pier and a sad-looking pirogue tied to a stump.

"Smell that? That's the swamp. Thick with souls. More souls in the swamp than anywhere else. See that pier? Tropical storm last fall tore it up. I was waiting for somebody to come fix it. Now I know I was waiting for y'all."

Phil is taken aback.

"We don't know how to fix piers. We, look, thanks for the coffee, but I gotta go get my muffler fixed."

Gus steps in.

"Madame Peychaud, don't listen to Phil. He's a little nervous but we can fix that pier for you."

"What!" gasps Phil. "We'll, we'll drown, we'll be eaten alive by, by leeches like in *The African Queen*. I'm a technical writer. I need all my fingers."

Madame Peychaud smiles at Phil benignly.

"Go ahead, baby, get your muffler. You don't have to do nothing you don't want to do."

* * *

Phil has taken the car to the nearest mechanic shop. Gus explores the oddities in the kitchen as Madame Peychaud speaks from another room. He stops to focus for

85

a moment on a photograph of a woman. It is the woman we know as the fairy queen, but Gus does not know her. He cocks his head to the side to read the diagonal inscription.

"One face, one voice, one habit"
Q. Mab

He steps away from the photograph and picks up a wooden akua-ma doll from Ghana.

"Hey," he calls out. "What's this wooden thing?"

"Wooden thing?" calls Madame Peychaud from the other room. "That must be your head, baby."

"No, it's like a little statue."

He holds it and studies it closely, not realizing that Madame Peychaud is now standing directing behind him. Her voice comes in a tone of inscrutable authority.

"Put that down!"

Gus jumps, puts it down, but continues his inquiry.

"What is it?"

"Akua-ma. Young woman long ago in Africa, barren. The priest tells her to make a wooden doll and take care of it like a baby, wash it, feed it, comfort it. And she does and next thing she has a beautiful baby girl. Ha, ha, ha."

"What's so funny?"

Madame Peychaud look at Gus dead-on, no longer laughing.

"I know what you thinking," she says.

Gus holds her gaze.

"Oh, what am I thinking?"

"Does she believe all this baloney. That's what you thinking."

She settles down into a chair at the kitchen table. Gus continues to stand.

"Ok, maybe that is what I'm thinking. It doesn't take ESP to know people's going to wonder if it's all BS."

"I know."

She gestures for Gus to sit down. He does. She puts some cut valerian root into a small mortar and begins grinding it into powder.

"Well, is it?" Gus asks.

"Is it what?"

"Is it all baloney?"

"Why you asking me? I thought you already decided?"

Gus is a little miffed that he has appeared unsure of his own skepticism.

"OK, well if you must know, I believe it's all magical hocus pocus. The priests do it to keep their power over the people, some people do it 'cause the truth's not enough for them, some people do it to … to make money."

She puts down the pestle.

"Is that what you think I'm about? Making money?"

Gus is a little ashamed. Too quick to act. Too quick to speak. He pulls himself in a little.

"No. I mean, I'm sorry. I know you mean well. But there's never been one piece of scientific evidence that any of this is true."

She puts the valerian powder into a tea ball.

"Ha, ha, ha. Science! Is that all you got?"

She moves to the stove, turns off a pot of boiling water, and puts the tea ball in, and begins walking around the room, touching the icons and objects until she reaches the doll.

"Imagination shows you more truth in five minutes than science shows you in 100 years. Look at that doll."

She pivots to eye Gus.

"Your people for thousands of years had that kind of connection to mother earth, that connection from blood to river, from heart to sky, to spirits in the earth everywhere. Some white man took all of that. And what did he give you? Science. A formula on a piece of paper. He looks at the river and sees H_2O. Your people looked at that same river and saw ancestors moving with gods, speaking to us in the sound of water, showing us things about the past and the future in every patch of foam breaking over the rocks. You gonna give all that away and take the H_2O. No imagination, no soul, just a formula. You might as well drain the blood right out of your body."

She takes out a spoon of the tea and offers it to Gus. He almost gags.

"What is that shit?"

"Valerian root."

Her voice is obscured by a thunderous crash as the rear screen door slams.

Madame Peychaud chuckles. She stands but does not move toward the door.

"Aren't you going to see who it is?" asks Gus.

She slaps a sign on the mantel. Gus is amazed that he has not seen the sign before. It reads:

MADAME PEYCHAUD
PSYCHIC GUIDE TO THE ANCIENTS
Past Life Regression, Numerology,
Iridology, Chakra Science

"I already know who it is," she says, giving the

88

sign a little secondary flick. After a pause, she adds: "Fool."

"What?"

"Not you, baby," she says to Gus. "That other fool."

She yells to the person in the other room.

"Claude, you loosening that spring?"

A Cajun accent comes from the other room.

"Poo-yie. You the sweetest mind reader in da world, Storm-Cherie." The speaker pronounces the name with the first two syllables unstressed, as if he wants to speed through them to get to the third syllable, whose rising stress gives the moniker a finish both affectionate and interrogative.

"Dass exactly what I'm doing."

"Told you when you put it in it was too tight."

The door slams a few more times, more gently now. Claude, a white Cajun a few years older than Madame Peychaud, toughened by hard work, walks in. His hair is thinning on top, with patches on the side like wings. His salt-and-pepper whiskers seem in a permanent state of stubble.

"Now how's dat?"

Madame Peychaud walks over and kisses him.

"That's better, baby."

"Who's your friend?"

"This is Gus," says Madame Peychaud. "He come to help us with the pier."

Claude looks at him with eyes a dark-roux brown. Warm eyes but piercing all the same.

"Ooh-ie. Just in time. I can't do it with my arthritis."

From the other direction, the front screen door slams. Phil enters, flustered.

89

"It's not just the muffler. It's broken exhaust hangers, and he needs new mounts to keep it from vibrating apart again. It's gonna take two days to get the parts."

"Dat ain't nuttin," says Claude. "Iss gonna take two week to built dat pier."

Chapter 8

The endless stream of crying cricket voices. The up rhythm. Then the down. The eternal sound of nature overhanging the bayou behind Madame Peychaud's shack. On the back porch of the shack, voices.

"What are we doing here, Gus?" Phil asks.

A raindrop falls close to the porch. So close, you could see it and smell it and hear it pop when it hit the ground. Then more raindrops. The big fat kind you get in Louisiana.

"Why are you on this goose chase looking for Hermia?" Phil continues, eyeing Gus.

Gus slides a galvanized steel bucket off the porch into the rain, just to hear the sound of water drops on metal.

"Why are you?" Gus replies.

Water pings the bucket. Faster and faster.

"I don't know. It seemed important. Hermia running off to her sister's. I figured we'd go find her and … and sort things out."

Gus is tapping the bucket with the handle of a broomstick. He doesn't seem to be paying attention. Then he speaks.

"What about Magnus?"

"I don't know," Phil says. "I guess I just wanted to know why he did it." He quietly freezes, realizing he had spoken to no one, not even Gus, about Magnus's crime.

"Did what?" Gus asks.

Phil squirms. His insides flutter.

"You know … why did he go with Hermia. Why things happened the way they did."

Gus does not reply.

Phil adds: "Just to put things together."

Gus runs the broom handle around the rim of the half-full bucket.

"You know what I think?" Gus says.

"What?"

"You just gotta do what's in front of you."

* * *

A sunny winter day in Louisiana can feel like a summer day somewhere else. Phil and Gus are in the water trying to work on the pier. Madame Peychaud watches from the back porch. Claude directs from above.

"Y'all gotta pull dat ole post out before you put da new one in."

Gus and Phil push and pull. The whole pier half collapses.

"Whee. Not like dat. Don't y'all built nothing back in the city?"

They fumble around. Claude suddenly jumps in and lifts the whole pier back into place. Phil and Gus shrink in comparison. Claude gets a temporary support in place, seats a new post, and jumps out.

"Like dat."

Gus and Phil go back to work, struggling with the

posts. Gus grumbles under his breath in the general direction of Claude.

"You sure you got arthritis?"

* * *

The table is set, and the four are eating in the shack: Madame Peychaud, Mr. Claude, Phil, and Gus. Mr. Claude, still chewing, addresses Phil.

"So what you do in dat jail?"

"Nothing. They had a Bible. I read a little."

"What you read?"

"New Testament. Something about the prophet Joel."

Madame Peychaud nods approval.

"God says through the Prophet Joel: 'I will pour my spirit into the world.'"

They pause at the drama in Madame Peychaud's voice. She turns to Claude.

"Gus here doesn't believe in the Bible and such hocus pocus."

"Oh yeah. Dis da scientist fella you told me about."

"I'm not a scientist," Gus says. "I'm a salesman."

Madame Peychaud continues.

"We all selling something."

The phrase reminds Gus of something, but he is in the midst of conversation and keeps going.

"I got nothing against reading the Bible," he says, "for inspiration. Just don't read it for facts."

Madame Peychaud is in her element now, enjoying the debate.

"Facts is dead husks, dead reminders of a bygone age, science just studies things as they was before God

92

poured his spirit into the world."

"But that makes no sense, Madame Peychaud. How can you have dead bodies before the spirit ever came into them?"

"Ha, ha. No, child. I'm not talking about chronological time. That's how science talks about time. I'm talking about the spiritual order of things. I'm talking about living reality, not dead reality."

Claude tugs Gus's elbow sympathetically.

"Gus, you might as well enjoy the catfish. You can't outtalk Storm-Cherie. She's a real talker."

Now Madame Peychaud turns to Phil.

"What you think, baby? You been quiet."

Phil measures his words before he speaks.

"I agree with Mr. Claude. If you can outtalk a pharmaceutical salesman, you're a real talker."

For a moment, it is unclear whether this is offensive or funny. Then they laugh.

* * *

It's not just crickets. Mosquitos are buzzing. Outboard motors occasionally drone and fade in the far distance. Nearer, one can hear every few minutes the "plip" of a fish jumping in the bayou or a turtle head going back under. Gus and Phil are struggling with the pier but making progress. Two young rednecks drift by in a pirogue.

"Hey, Bubba, look at them guys by dat pier. Dey ain't from around here."

"No, Billy, I never seen 'em."

"Hey," shouts Billy. "What y'all doing?"

Gus and Phil are concentrating. Billy shouts again.

"That ain't no way to fix a pier."

93

Now Bubba joins in.

"I could beat that post in with a mush melon faster'n that, couillon."

Billy and Bubba laugh. Gus finally responds.

"It might be faster if we beat your head against the post to get it in."

The laughter from the pirogue grows more robust. Billy calls back.

"How you gonna catch us?"

Gus looks around. His eyes light upon Madame Peychaud's old pirogue.

The boys in the boat miss nothing.

"You couldn't catch us in dat ole boat for a hundred dollars."

Gus indiscreetly goes taunt for taunt.

"A hundred dollars says we can."

The boys confer on the boat for a moment.

"Next Saturday," says Billy. "We race y'all from Theriot's Marina to Padeaux's Pier in Delcambre. And bring your $100."

Phil whispers.

"No, Gus."

Gus hesitates.

"Don't do it," comes the whisper.

Gus calls to the boat.

"Alright, we'll be there. Theriot's Marina."

The boys chuckle and paddle away with graceful speed.

Gus turns to Phil.

"Come on, Phil. You can't let guys get away with that shit."

"I know," says Phil glumly.

"Look," concedes Gus. "We don't have to do it if you don't want."

94

Phil looks out over the bayou that fades into swamp. Turtles sun on a log. A great blue heron wades in the shallows.

"OK, Gus. Let's do it."

* * *

In the Bourbon Street cottage, the fairy queen has finished steaming her face in the sink. She is reapplying her makeup.

* * *

Days go by at Madame Peychaud's shack. Phil and Gus alternate between work on the pier and bumbling through test runs in the boat.

* * *

The fairy queen finishes her makeup, straightens her costume, and steps out of the cottage and into the street, into the phantasmagoria of mock-identity and excess that is Mardi Gras.

* * *

Phil, Gus, Madame Peychaud, and Mr. Claude sit at the kitchen table in the shack. It is Saturday morning, time to go to Theriot's Marina. Claude rallies the team.

"You boys have a shot a whiskey with y'all coffee. You gonna need it."

Gus pours shots and attempts to pour one for Claude, too, but Claude gestures it away."

"He doesn't drink," says Madame Peychaud.

95

"Gave it up months ago."

She kisses him. He is eager to change the subject.

"Storm-Cherie, gimme them coffee grinds."

He dumps the wet grinds on the table and they form a circle about 4-5 inches in diameter. He takes out a screwdriver as a pointer to map what he is about to say.

"Theriot's Marina is here. Bayou Lafarge curve around like dis till it gets to Delcambre. Now over here is a shortcut through dat cypress swamp. I know dem boys gonna try to cheat and go true dem swamp. But I know dat route good as dey know dat route."

He lays the screwdriver down.

"You let me take care of da swamp. You go fass and time dey get outa dat swamp you be in Delcambre."

Theriot's Marina, the first stop of the day, is a shack not unlike Madame Peychaud's shack, but with more open space for lounging and politicking and horsing around. The two boats for the race are decorated up with colorful triangular pennants, balloons, and mock camouflage of mosses and duck boat stencils. Curiosity and excitement show in the onlookers on the banks. The Cajun boys are taunting in earnest, encouraging the spectators to join in.

Mr. Claude is master of ceremonies.

"Now y'all agree da race follows da Bayou Lafarge around to Padeaux's Pier in Delcambre. No messing with each other along da way and no shortcuts. Dass right?"

Billy and Bubba agree: "Dass right."

Phil and Gus concur: "Right."

Without further warning, Claude pulls out a pistol and shoots in the air.

The race is on. Both teams have moments of high seriousness and moments of laughter. The Cajuns are eventually too far ahead to be seen. Billy looks back to verify that the other boat is lost to sight.

"OK, Bubba, there's the shortcut through the cypress swamp."

"We don't need the shortcut, Billy. We a mile ahead of 'em."

"I know we don't need it, Bubba, but it'll save us a whole hour. We won't break a sweat and we'll beat 'em ten times worse. The secret ain't just to win, the secret's to make'm feel lower'n a snake belly in a wagon rut."

They cut into the cypress swamp.

At another part of the bayou, Phil and Gus are paddling. Gus is having second thoughts.

"Shit, Phil. I know I talk before I think. How we gonna out-canoe a bunch a Cajuns been wrestling alligators since they were two years old."

"Forget it, Gus. Let's just take our time. It's fun. $100 swamp tour."

They relax a little bit and enjoy the flora and fauna at a slower pace.

Little do they know that the Cajun boys are getting tangled in two or three nonlethal booby traps that Claude had set up in the cypress swamp. Unaware of this advantage that might be pressed, Phil and Gus paddle more leisurely. Gus points into the swamp that forms what would otherwise be the banks of the bayou.

"Look! Real alligators!"

Phil gets up. They smile at the sight. With both standing, the pirogue starts to rock. Then it flips. Gus comes up and rights the boat. Before he can get in, he notices Phil has not come up.

* * *

On a still black bayou a blue heron sits silently on a cypress knee. The water, though, is most still. Eternally still.

* * *

Gus dives into the still waters frantically.

Chapter 9

The Cajun rednecks, frustrated, are now hitting their last booby trap. They break loose and re-enter the bayou at its widest in distant sight of Padeaux's. A small crowd is waiting, cheering them on.

"Wait, Billy!" cries Bubba. "Look! It's dem city boys."

Gus and Phil's pirogue approaches from the main artery of the bayou. Phil is wrapped in a blanket and Gus is paddling with all he's got. The two boats approach evenly for a while, then the rednecks' boat slowly begins to go downward as well as forward.

"Whass wrong, Billy?"

"I don't know."

Billy rummages around with his hand below the water line inside the boat.

"Shit!" Billy says. "That last booby trap punched a hole in the boat."

"Shit!" says Bubba.

Phil and Gus drift up to Padeaux's pier in Delcambre. They land and the crowd bursts into celebration.

* * *

Hosts and guests scamper across Padeaux's patio in preparation for the Saturday night fais-do-do. Some friendly locals have taken Phil and Gus on a victory run around the bayou, visiting legendary sites of star-crossed love between Coushatta natives and French settlers, old sunken boats purportedly from pirate days, and a floating bar on a houseboat with no shortage of customers despite being so far removed from any trace of civilization that it seems to sprout up from the exotic ecosystem itself. Now the bayou tour is over and the sun is setting at Padeaux's. Frogs croak, crickets hum, a lizard pauses its run along on the fence to take note of human voices. An old Cajun trio tunes up. Gus and Phil sit at a picnic table. Gus is drinking a beer and Phil is re-wrapped in his blanket, drinking a hot elixir of honey, lemon, hot water, and Jack Daniels.

"Never thought it would turn out so good, eh Phil? I guess this is jambalaya, crawfish pie, filé gumbo."

"And here comes the snapping turtle," says Phil sourly.

Billy and Bubba walk up.

"Y'all got our hundred dollars?" asks Billy.

"We won," says Gus.

Billy looks at Bubba.

"Did they win, Bubba?"

"They won but they cheated, Billy. Way I see it, that ain't rightly winning at all."

Billy looks back at the picnic table.

"Bubba here says you won but you cheated."

He turns.

"What's that mean, Bubba?"

"I don't know, Billy. Does that mean we do'm like we done the Chaisson brothers?"

Billy stays focused on Phil and Gus.

"What Bubba here is trying to say - in his own retarded way - is that you gotta take a ass-whipping before you get your $100."

Two additional country boys, one with a bat, join the Cajun rednecks. Things are looking bad.

Gus puts his beer to the side.

"One way or another ..." Gus says. He stands up boldly. Phil stumbles to his feet shakily, still wrapped in the blanket. Gus finishes his sentence.

"... we'll take our $100."

The bat-wielder smashes Gus and Phil's table. Gus and Billy engage. Claude appears from nowhere.

"Billy, you nuts?" he shouts.

In an exhilarating show of anger and power, Claude knocks the foursome into disarray, grabs the bat, and holds Billy down against the picnic table with the bat at his throat. He seems in real danger of killing Billy, and Gus, afraid that might happen, gestures to call Claude off. Claude calms down as Billy gasps.

"You wait till T-Bone hears about this," says Claude. Billy is deflated.

"Aw, Mr. Claude, don't tell T-Bone. T-Bone's my parrain."

"T-Bone stick dat bat up yo' ass, Billy."

"Please don't tell T-Bone, Mr. Claude. We didn't mean nothing."

"Y'all give dem fellas dey $100. And give Mr. Padeaux $100 for dat table."

The boys confer, and Billy sheepishly delivers the results of the conference.

"But Mr. Claude, we only got $100."

"You give it to dese boys. And get outa here and don't come back till you got Mr. Padeaux's money."

They give over the $100 to Gus.

Claude welcomes Gus and Phil into the middle of the party.

"Y'all come on."

They enter the party, and the scene ramps up with accordions and fiddles, washboards and bucket drums, Cajun dancing and hard drinking late into the night.

* * *

All is quiet behind Madame Peychaud's shack. Gus and Claude sit on the pier.

"Mr. Claude, you scared the hell out of me tonight when you grabbed that bat."

"Scared myself a little."

The two men gaze across the bayou.

"You gonna tell T-Bone, Mr. Claude?"

"No. I once learned the hard way don't kill your enemy unless you have to. Just slow 'em down a bit, and then help 'em back up. People's funny. Worst enemy might turn out to be on your side one day."

"Is that why you don't drink? Afraid you might kill your enemy?"

"Something like dat. Y'all take care. I gotta go git dem trap I lay for dem boys out da swamp."

He hops in the pirogue and glides gracefully away. Gus looks up at the stars. Madame Peychaud comes out of the back door of the house and approaches Gus.

"Look at all them stars. Something happening. Something breaking loose. You feel it?"

"You know I don't feel it. I'm not sure you feel it."

"Oh, yeah," says Madame Peychaud. "You don't believe in the stars."

"I believe in the stars. I just don't believe they have any magical power over me. That's all in your mind."

"Amen," she agrees.

"You mean you admit it's all in your mind?"

"Sure it is, baby. Ain't no difference between mind and body."

"What's that mean?"

"You don't believe in the stars."

"I do believe…" Gus starts in.

She shushes him.

"How about some coffee?"

"Sure."

They begin to walk to the back door. Madame Peychaud muses out loud.

"All the stars up there just part of our big body."

Gus replies in form as they reach the door.

"My body is made up of cells. Blood cells, brain cells. Cells."

102

They enter. Gus sits at the table and Madame Peychaud walks to the stove and returns with a pot of coffee and a cup for Gus. She fills the cup.

"Your body made up of cells, huh baby?"

"Yeah. Thanks for the coffee."

"Your mind made up of them same cells. All your little brain cells and blood cells got their bumps and sways and turns. Every one of those bumps and sways and turns affects the mind. The body is the mind. Changes in the body is changes in the mind. Just like with the big body stretching right up through the sky with all them stars."

"Sort of like cellular astrology."

"That's right! That's exactly right! Like cellular astrology. You got a sharp mind, baby. Now you starting to see there's more to science than you ever thought. You starting to bring science out of its trap. You looking at it whole – mental, emotional, spiritual, physical."

"That sounds like something Magnus said. The four sheaths."

Madame Peychaud is stunned. She looks at Gus as if seeing him for the first time.

"You do know about the four sheaths?" asks Gus, unsure of what triggered the change in Madame Peychaud. Unsure of where he is leading. Or being led.

Madame Peychaud slaps the promotional sign.

"Of course, I know about the four sheaths."

Gus is thinking hard.

"Do you know Magnus, Madame Peychaud?"

"Yeah, I know him. See this picture?"

She takes down the picture of the woman Gus had seen earlier and places it on the table.

"You know her?" she asks.

"No."

"That's Maggie Leblanc. You never heard of Maggie Leblanc?"

"I think Magnus mentioned her once."

"Good. 'Cause she don't mention him to me no more."

Madame Peychaud hangs the picture back up. As she returns to the table, Phil stumbles in hung over, eavesdropping on the conversation in progress.

"Maggie and I were collecting oils and potions," says Madame Peychaud.

Phil, who has missed the entire show and tell scene, mumbles to himself in a daze: "Maggie?!"

Madame Peychaud continues with Gus, inattentive to Phil.

"Had a whole tray full. Precious oils and potions. When Magnus came it was great at first."

Phil still mumbles to himself.

"Magnus?!"

She continues.

"He was an added inspiration. It was like a spiritual garden in the swamp. And then he left like a thief in the night. And Maggie..."

She drifts into a silent reverie. Phil enters the conversation.

"Did, did Maggie know about this ..."

Madame Peychaud glares at him and he tries to finish as quickly and vaguely as possible.

"This … whatever it is that Magnus did?"

"Maggie knows. But she ain't a snake like Magnus. She'll come clean one day."

"Unless," ponders Phil.

"Unless what?"

"Unless … she can't come clean."

"You don't make any sense," says Madame Peychaud. "Now y'all get out. Our business is finished here."

* * *

Phil's car rumbles down a densely wooded road. Gus speaks as he tries to wind the tape back into a cassette.

"What do you mean you lost your bean at Madame Peychaud's?"

"My fava bean. It's good luck."

"You have a good luck bean?"

"Not just me. It's a Catholic thing. Sicilian, I think. It's from the St. Joseph's altar."

"Well that makes me feel better. It's a religious bean."

The blackness shudders as the first patches of dawn appear. Gus breaks into a snore. It is a quiet snore but loud enough to wake himself up. He jumps. He rubs his eyes, works his jaw.

"I wonder how Magnus got Madame Peychaud so worked up anyway."

"Like she said, he's a snake."

"Damn, Phil, you ain't over that yet?"

Gus rolls the window down half way. The air is damp. The whole world seems damp.

"I thought you were over that."

"You know what?" Phil replies. "Fuck Magnus. Fuck Magnus and fuck Madame Peychaud. It's Mardi Gras this Tuesday. I got no job. And you know what? I was just starting to feel good about that. So fuck them. It's carnival time."

He adjusts his left buttock.

"We're going to New Orleans."

Chapter 10

At the Wheat Seed Health Food Store, Phil is in lively discussion with Ginger. His handheld basket holds two bottles of pomegranate juice. Leeza approaches and calls out.

"Hey, Phil! Where were y'all? Magnus and Hermia were looking for y'all. Magnus wanted to see you before he left town."

"Magnus?! He was in town? Where's he going?"

"He wouldn't say. But he asked if I thought you'd mind if he stored some stuff at your house."

"At MY house?! What did you say?"

"I said you're his brother. Of course, you wouldn't mind. So I gave him my spare key."

Phil, flustered, wants to change the subject. He needs time to think.

"Who, who's going to run the wellness center if Magnus leaves?"

Leeza holds up a set of keys and smiles.

"You and me. Magnus said the cash flow is ours."

"What cash flow? He couldn't even keep his car from getting repossessed."

"Oh, that? No, he paid it all off."

"What?! Why would he lie to me about that?"

"Why does Magnus lie about anything?"

Leeza delivers this rhetorical question with a "duh" look, as if to say, "Don't you know Magnus by now?"

Phil stammers.

"Well, well that still doesn't give us any cash flow for the Sunspot. How many months behind are we, anyway?"

"Don't be such a worrywart, Phil," said Leeza. Then, as an afterthought: "Oh, Phil, Magnus said he left something for you with Maggie."

Phil's consternation is reaching the breaking point. Why would Magnus say such a thing? He killed Maggie. He left something with Maggie. Could Magnus be one of those perfect psychopaths, like the psychotic Dr. Schreber in Freud's case history – brilliant and charismatic in all things external but hideously sick inside?

Phil thinks of the card from Rex. *If you ever need anything.* This is what it meant! Fate had intended it. He would go to Rex, borrow the money to get things right. And he would find out, one way or another, what Magnus had left with Maggie. Or whatever he meant by that.

"What's the matter, Phil?" Leeza cuts in. "Do you know how to reach Maggie?"

Phil ponders. How do you reach across that fabled chasm between the living and the dead? He smiles. Checks himself for smiling. Maybe, he thinks, *I am the psychopath.*

"Phil!" says Leeza more firmly.

"No, no, I don't know how to reach Maggie," he says.

"But I'm going to find out."

* * *

The fairy queen wanders the French Quarter amidst Mardi Gras revelers. She sees a reveler costumed as the elephant god, Ganesh, remover of obstacles, in front of the Napoleon House.

You must find the elephant-man.

She tries to navigate through the crowd, but he is gone by the time she arrives.

* * *

In a sea of fluorescent light from drop-ceiling panels, dull gray divider walls and stackable plastic desk organizers, Phil approaches his old cubicle. Jerry is happy to see him.

"Hey, brahmachari. How's the love life?"

"Actually, Jerry, quite good. Better than ever."

"Wow! Who is she ... or he?"

"As Walt Whitman almost said, 'The world is my orgasm.'"

"Wow, Phil! You're Studio 54 all over. You looking for work?"

"Not here."

Finn comes over at the sound of Phil's voice.

"Hey-hey, lover boy! Did you use the guy code on that bloodsucker?"

"Yeah, and I learned a new corollary to the guy code."

"Oh yeah! What's that?"

Phil leans in confidentially.

"Don't say, 'Fuck you, you fucking fuck,' unless you really mean it."

"What?"

"So I'm telling you, Finn, right here and now: 'Fuck you, you fucking fuck!'"

Finn is taken aback "Whaaat?"

Phil peers into Finn's face viciously, then breaks.

"Just pissing in your sink, Finn."

Finn begins to see that it's a joke.

"What?"

"Gotcha!" says Phil.

Finn laughs. Phil pokes his ribs.

Phil walks toward the door with his box of personal items. "Way to go, tiger!" Jerry calls from far away.

* * *

The office appears in smart, clean geometrical shapes, nothing like the cubicles where Phil had worked. Phil sits in the waiting room, looking at the mysterious door:

Rex Enterprises
T. Rex, President

Phil thinks about what he would say. He really has no collateral. All he has to go on is Rex's offer. *If you ever need anything*. Did Rex really know Hermia? Phil had not heard her speak of him. Did he have his own designs on Hermia? No. Probably just a rich guy, patron of the arts and whatnot.

"You may go in now."

Phil enters. Mr. Rex, an imposing figure a couple

of years older than Magnus, stands up from behind the broad desk.

"Well, hello there," says Rex. "The young man from the art show. With Hermia, no?"

He stares at Phil with the same knowing look from the art show.

"Do you know me?" he asks.

The question flusters Phil.

"No, but when I met you, you, you said…"

Rex sees Phil's anxiety and calms him.

"No, no, I don't mind you coming here at all. It's just that I can't help but think I've seen your face before. Were you ever at Tulane? Maybe the Southern Yacht Club?"

Phil humbly nixes the possibility of a meeting at those fine establishments, and Rex seems satisfied. He sees many faces in his business after all.

"What can I do for you?"

Phil introduces himself, reminds Rex of his comment at the art show, of the business card he had kept ever since. *If you ever need anything*. He explains that his sister and he have a wellness center – always been successful mind you, but in a temporary jam.

"Sure, we might be able to help," says Rex. He runs his hand over his slick black hair and smiles. Is it the smile of a businessman? Of a philanthropist? Of a primeval predator? How could you tell the difference?

"I have some numbers," says Phil. "It's not much really. But my brother, Magnus, he kept the books, and …"

Phil notes that Rex is not paying attention. His face has a funny look.

"That's it!" interrupts Rex.

"That's where I've seen your face. You're

Magnus's little brother."

"Yes, yes!" exclaims Phil, relieved that a personal connection might take some of the pressure off of his flimsy solicitation.

"Yes, Magnus," repeats Phil, trying to hold back his glee.

"Where is Magnus?" asked Rex.

"I don't know. He disappeared."

Rex takes a cigar from a cigar box.

"Good for you," says Rex. "Get rid of the rats."

Phil's glee is turning to apprehension.

"Did Magnus ever tell you about the old irons works?" asks Rex.

"In our old neighborhood?" queries Phil. "No, he never said much about it."

"No, you were too young to run around the neighborhood," says Rex. "Magnus probably thought nothing of the old iron works, but I remember, loud and clear."

"Loud and clear" seems to Phil an odd way to remember things, but he thinks best to keep his mouth shut and see where things are going.

"I learned a lesson that day that made me who I am," says Rex. "About rats. About not letting your guard down and getting hustled."

Rex lit his cigar and closed his eyes for a moment as the puff of smoke floated upward.

* * *

Two boys roam the old iron works. Bits and pieces of heavy machinery litter the dirt floor. Overhead, giant metal rafters and broken windows. Something glistens in the dirt. The older boy reaches down, dusts it off, pulls it from

111

where it had stuck gently in the earth floor. An iron rod a few inches long with a bow at one end and a solid bit like a tiny flag at the other. A skeleton key. Where the rod meets the bow, the boy can almost make out a figure, perhaps a monk, that had been carved into the key long ago and had now faded almost into oblivion.

"Let me see," says the younger boy. As he reaches out, the older boy is suddenly tempted to pull it back and not have it seen by the other. But too late. The younger has plucked it from the hand of the older and looks at it in wonder. They run outside to the sidewalk in front of the iron works to see their treasure in the sunlight. As they do, they crash into something. A big person. Well, a teenager at least, with long curly hair. One of the long-haired boys that had started hanging around the neighborhood. Some new thing called the hippie movement.

"Y'all better watch out for rats in there," says the teenager. "And those old rusty pipes. You don't want to cut yourself in that place."

"We can play wherever we want," says the older boy.

"Sure you can," smiles the teenager. "But you don't want to end up the hospital like the Bamberly brothers."

As the mysterious brothers in question give pause to the older boy, the younger, who is, truth be told, not as ill-natured as the older, offers the skeleton key for the teenager's view.

"Look what we found in there," he says.

The teenager inspects it.

"Nice find," he says. "What y'all gonna do with it?"

"We're gonna sell it for a hundred dollars," says the older boy.

"What would you do with a hundred dollars?" smiles the teenager.

"We could get ..." The older boy pauses. He hasn't quite thought that far.

"Ice cream," says the younger.

"Yeah, ice cream," says the older. Secretly he wants much more than ice cream, but he can't think of anything to say.

"I tell you what," says the teenager. "You give me the key, and I'll give you two dollars for ice cream. I'll take the key to Mr. Booth at the locksmiths and get it cleaned and oiled and bring it here tomorrow, same place, same time."

"Sure," says the younger and handed over the key.

The boys enjoy their ice cream, but when the teenager does not come back the next day, things turn bad. The older boy, although he has shared in the spoils of the ice cream, starts thinking that the younger was entirely responsible for the loss of his treasure, after he – he himself – had found it buried. He starts thinking that the deal with the teenager was done against his will. He imagines how he had resisted but the teenager and Magnus had betrayed him. Magnus especially. The teenager had stolen the goods but Magnus had been the traitor within. Tyler would never trust anyone again. He would get his hundred dollars – a million dollars – and no one would ever betray him again without paying for it.

Magnus, meanwhile, enjoyed his ice cream and kept faith in the teenager. Something happened, but he would come back. In fact, Magnus had heard sirens near the old iron works that night. Yes, that was it. The teenager had got into some kind of trouble, but he would come back.

"I'll give you something," says Rex. "A piece of advice. Help people who help you back. Now get out."

Phil stumbles out onto the street of the central business district. He is dazed. The sun blazes. How could the sun blaze at this time of year? Phil is not sure what is real and what is not. But Maggie. He could still try to find Maggie. Or whatever Maggie left behind.

* * *

It looks like a machine from a scientific laboratory. Or maybe a medical research center. A large box assembly with a vertical screen. Protruding from the bottom, a cylindrical lens hovers over a flat surface of glass. The glass slides out and pivots upward to 45 degrees. A hand rolls a narrow sheet of black film under the glass and flips a power switch. The microfilm is now visible on the vertical screen.

The room, it turns out, is neither a scientific laboratory nor a medical research center. It is the genealogy room at the New Orleans Public Library. Phil's telephone book research and calls to Leblanc families having utterly failed, the genealogy room is his last-ditch effort.

Phil had remembered those words Magnus spoke – years ago it seemed – at the Pirate's Alley café with Hermia and Gus and the Romanian waiter, in the damp river air. It seemed a tense night back then, but now that night seems the good old days. Funny how perspectives change. But Phil had remembered.

She's younger than you, little brother

She couldn't be too much younger. Magnus was four years older than Phil. He couldn't be dating anyone much younger.

from a faraway empire like Gus

That had raised Gus's words from Laura's restaurant to recollection.

Hell no, my people's from New York.

New York. The Empire State. Maggie was from New York. Phil had come to the genealogy room for days in a row, missing the big carnival parades this week before Fat Tuesday – Babylon and Hermes and Momus – searching newspapers from the early 1970s, years that would have included Maggie's early childhood and possibly her birth. And indeed, he had found one blurry photo in *The Daily Freeman* newspaper of Northern Dutchess County. It was dated to 1973 with the caption, "Maggie Leblanc, 2, sleeps in her mother's arms as local circus performers soar." With an aerial performance in progress in the background, the child was swaddled up like a mummy. Another child, maybe four, was swinging herself around in wild communion with the performance at hand. The mother, lovely and strong-jawed, smooth shoulder showing a tiny rose tattoo, was clearly African-American. This had surprised Phil, but he remained focused. If that were Maggie, she would have been born in late 1970 or early 1971. If her birth was recorded, her parents would be too.

Phil now cranks the spindle, moving the strip of

film across the screen. In the microforms library, it was surprisingly easy to get birth records from every hospital in Dutchess County. All but one: The Hudson River State Hospital, which had been shuttered and merged with another hospital in 1994. Phil takes the forwarding phone number and heads out.

* * *

The fairy queen stands in front of the Napoleon House. Costumed characters wheel past. A mermaid, a tin man, a bearded nun. She closes her eyes. She is a little girl again. She sits in a circle, a pony ring it seems, with several other children but no ponies. One of the children holds something curled in her hand, a great treasure by all appearances. Girls and boys gather round. The child with the treasure is Maggie's best friend, a sister, a girl with brown skin and creole green eyes. She opens her hand to reveal the prize: an old skeleton key, a gift from a hand long ago. A grown woman's voice calls and breaks the spell.

* * *

"If you hold just a minute, I'll get you Marge. She's the only one here who came over from the Hudson River State Hospital when we merged in 1994."

Phil holds on. The last hospital in Dutchess County. There had to be a Leblanc. This Marge must remember. The county can't be more than 10% black, so Phil had that in his favor, too. Marge must remember.

"Marge speaking."

Phil inquires cautiously. Marge is equally cautious.

116

"I'm looking for a family or baby named Leblanc. The baby would have been born in late 1970 or early 1971. Were you at the Hudson River Hospital then?"

"Yes, but there weren't any babies born there."

"No babies born in the whole year at the hospital?!"

"Don't be so shocked," Marge says sourly. "It was a psyc hospital. Any maternities would have been sent to Hyde Park."

Now Phil is discouraged.

"I'm sorry. I didn't know."

Phil is at a loss.

"It's just ... my family ... I don't know."

His despair triggers some empathy, and Marge expands her brain activity beyond the conventional box into which she normally fits everything.

"Wait, did you say, Leblanc?"

"Yes, Leblanc," says Phil with a glimmer of hope.

"I remember now. A young woman. Jazmine Leblanc."

"Did she have a baby?"

"No. No baby."

"Well, but," Phil stammers. "How do you know?"

"It was a psyc hospital. No one had babies here."

"But maybe she'd had a child before."

"No, I remember Jazmine. There was no child."

"But maybe she'd had a baby before."

"No. I'd know if she had ever had a baby."

"How would you know for sure?"

Marge was turning sour again.

"It was a medical facility, sir. We did keep medical histories of our patients."

"But maybe she had a baby later."

"You'd have to ask Hyde Park."

117

No good. Phil had already asked Hyde Park. This was his last hospital. He soldiered on.

"Well, well, was she African-American?"

But now Marge begins to feel she has said too much.

"I can't give you any more medical information, sir."

"But, but …" Phil is pleading. He will lie, cheat, do anything.

"There's a family here suffering, ma'am. A young woman. She just needs to know a bit about her birth mother. If we can even rule out this Jazmine Leblanc as the birth mother, it would give so much relief to the family."

Marge bends.

"Well, I can tell you one thing," Marge says.

"Yes?"

"Mind you, I'm not giving medical information."

"Yes, I'm minded, I know. Yes? Yes?"

"I remember Jazmine clear as day. Sweet girl."

"Sweet girl. Yes, I'm sure she was. And?"

"And she was white as snow. This is definitely not your Leblanc family."

* * *

The fairy queen dreams. She is back at the pony ring, but it must be a year or two later. Maroon paint is chipping from the low concrete sitting wall at the perimeter of the ring. There is a door at the edge of the pony ring. A small puppet house. A small door. Maggie must get the door open. She must do it. She grasps the knob in her small fist. She pulls. It does not open. She laughs. She knows what will happen. She pulls again and again, to no avail, laughing, her little head bobbing to and fro. Pulling, pulling so hard that her hands slide through the door knob and she plops back on the ground. Then the door bursts open and the girl with brown skin and creole green eyes, pops out, laughing, laughing. But the laughter dissipates. Maggie remembers that last day, leaving the farm, her home, seeing the pony ring fade in the distance, the leaves on the trees rumpling in the wind.

* * *

Phil is writing at the desk in his apartment. Someone knocks at the door. Gus's voice comes through.

"Come on, Phil. It's Mardi Gras Day! Fat Tuesday!"

"No. I'm gonna stay in. I'm working on something. What you doing?"

"Going to St Charles with some old pharm rep friends."

"Watch your wallet."

"Alright then."

A motorcycle cranks and Gus leaves.

Phil turns back to his desk, his work, a poem, in pen and ink. He finishes. He cocks his head back an inch or so to review his work.

In Memory of Maggie Leblanc

Separate they sit on the stone
a lizard below flashing green and gray
the sleek soft body coiled in fear
or hatred or worse. Monuments surround them.

The horizon ruptures, up, up
it floats and hangs through the moss
mislaid dreams of a fruitful season
their own bodies sleek and soft and coiled.

I see her now clear and separate
fading fingers fine-strung in moss
and behind her the radish slice moon
all beauty and light and bitter ash.

The creative process was intense and visceral, and Phil likes the poem – on its internal merits – but it doesn't suit. It doesn't match up right to anything he wants to say about Maggie or Magnus or anyone else. The more he likes the poem, the more it misses any connection to his life. All imagination. What's wrong with imagination?

Phil tears up paper in frustration, looks around, notices Magnus's lavish Ganesh Mardi Gras costume – the silky red balloon pants, the bobble head and elephant trunk, bejeweled blue body. This sportive simulacrum of the pensive Hindu god is newly hung up in the corner above some boxes marked "Magnus - books," "Magnus - supplies," etc. Phil whispers as he looks at the costume.

"Magnus."

He slowly approaches and methodically dons the costume, piece by piece, in mock-heroic echo of Homer's "arming of the warrior."

120

On the streets of the French Quarter, Mardi Gras is now in full flower, and Phil, Ganesh, the elephant man wanders the scene. He stands for a moment in front of the Napoleon House. Then he enters and sits at the bar.

He orders a drink, sits more contemplative than festive. He thinks of Hermia. She was good. She deserved more. And of Magnus, impenetrable. And the long night drives through swamps and rice farms with Gus. The crazy meeting with Madame Peychaud and Mr. Claude. He had damn near drowned in that bayou. For what? He hears a voice.

"Elephant man."

Phil freezes for a second. He hears the voice but the speaker is behind him unseen.

"I know you."

Phil turns to face the fairy queen.

"You know me?"

Now the fairy queen is herself startled. She holds two fingers to her throat and speaks in a muted voice.

"I don't know you."

"But you recognize my costume. This is Magnus's costume. You know Magnus."

"I know Magnus."

"Where is he?"

Fairy Queen takes a stool by Phil. She doesn't answer.

"Who are you?"

She thinks for a moment.

"I'm the fairy queen."

"So, fairy queen, how do you know Magnus?"

"He owes me a birthday cake."

"So you're! Wait! I saw a birthday cake. It was for Queen Mab."

The fairy queen smiles. Phil senses things taking

an eerie turn.

"Ah, Queen Mab," she says.

"Do you know Queen Mab?"

"I am Queen Mab."

"Wait. You can't be Queen Mab. I always thought Queen Mab was Maggie…"

He cuts off, afraid he is saying too much.

"Maggie Leblanc," says the fairy queen, interrogatively.

"Yes, yes, Maggie Leblanc."

Phil shuts up again, afraid of his own conversation.

"Do you know Maggie Leblanc?" asks the fairy queen.

"I've never met her but I know Magnus was … close to her."

"Ah," she says. "Close to her. Very close, would you say?"

Phil closes his eyes, quietly panicking.

* * *

A black corvette speeds down a country road.

* * *

Phil opens his eyes and looks earnestly at the fairy queen.

"Who are you? How do you know Magnus?"

"Ah, Magnus," she says. "He lived it. Like Zorba the Greek. Dancing it every minute."

"What do you mean, 'He lived,' 'He was.' Where is he? You know, don't you?"

* * *

122

The black corvette continues its flight.

* * *

"Even with Hermia," continues the fairy queen. "Always doing the dance."

Phil is getting agitated.

"Who gives a shit about Hermia? Where's my brother?"

The fairy queen stares into Phil's eyes.

"Stay focused, Phil. We're all on this path. You and Hermia walked this path together. Human contact is the most powerful form of yoga."

Background voices in the bar become excited as a TV behind the bar shows a black corvette being chased on a country highway by police cars.

"Hey, look at this car chase," calls a one-eyed-jack bar patron to his friend back at the table. "That guy's hauling ass."

Phil and the fairy queen continue their conversation, not yet aware of the car chase.

"That sounds like something Magnus would say," Phil says.

"I know."

The fairy queen smiles. Phil sips his drink. The fairy queen continues.

"The past isn't gone, Phil. It's still here like all the rings of a tree are still here. Invisible till the tree falls, but here all the while. Tread softly for those who fall."

Phil turns to her. His voice is more withdrawn.

"Where is Hermia?"

Excitement builds over the TV car chase. Phil and the fairy queen take notice, especially Phil when he sees the corvette.

"They say it's in Terrebonne Parish," calls the one-eyed jack. "The cops are all over this guy."

Phil quietly panics as the TV shows barriers being set up across the highway. The speeding black corvette enters the picture.

Phil mumbles under his breath.

"Magnus!"

The black corvette crashes spectacularly into the barriers in a white lightning flash. Phil is stunned. He collapses off stool.

Chapter 11

In the neatly decorated bedroom of the fairy queen, Phil lies unconscious on the bed. His elephant mask is off to the side. The fairy queen, mask off, opens the shirt of his costume and dabs oils on his chest.

Phil awakes, sees in a groggy haze the fairy queen's beaming face sans mask.

"You are Maggie Leblanc," he monotones.

"Yes, I am Maggie Leblanc."

They contemplate for a moment, she beaming, he in a daze.

"But Magnus killed Maggie Leblanc."

The fairy queen smiles. Phil stirs and half raises himself.

"Magnus couldn't kill a fly," she says.

"But Magnus said …"

"You know Magnus, Phil. Always pushing people to the next step."

"But Madame Peychaud said ..."

"Ha, ha, ha." The fairy queen does not smile this time. She laughs. She literally laughs. Her voice sounds strange with that much air in it.

"Madame Peychaud," she says, her laugh coming down to a chuckle. "Now there's somebody who could kill a fly or two."

She gets up and walks to the shelf that holds a number of small Egyptian bottles of varied shapes and colors. "Wait," Phil says suddenly. "You know Madame Peychaud?"

"Of course, I know Madame Peychaud," she says.

Phil, chastened, feels as if he missed something obvious.

"How do you think..." Maggie began and then stopped short.

Seeing Maggie hesitate allows Phil to regain some measure of self-assurance.

"How do you know Madame Peychaud?" he asks calmly.

Maggie opens one of the little Egyptian bottles and rubs the new oil between her fingers, releasing a scent both sharp and soothing.

"Madame Peychaud and I were going to set up an essential oils business."

Maggie turns back to Phil and adjusts her seat. Phil makes to sit up. She gently pushes him back down.

"Relax. Don't move just yet."

Maggie closes her eyes and thinks back.

"She knew the swamp and I knew the principles of essential oils. We were going to do regional essences: cypress, black pepper, sugar cane extract. We'd been collecting samples. I could feel a twitch and sometimes a burning in my palate. I could feel my lungs and throat failing. But we kept collecting. Mr. Claude hadn't been around for a few weeks. Then he came in one night. Drunk. Magnus had put all the oils on Claude's bed and was in his sleeping bag on the floor. Magnus had a thing about sleeping on the floor. This is the first Claude had seen of Magnus and he blew up. Claude was very pure, but very physical. And Magnus was in a very ethereal phase. It was like Claude was trying violently to absorb Magnus into the physical sheath. He could have killed Magnus in one blow. Then he turned suddenly and knocked everything off his bed, breaking all the flasks, and sat there with his head in his hands, from sudden violence to sudden despair. When Magnus stood up, I swear he had no substance, he was like a shadow or a ghost. And I was in the doorway thinking, 'Magnus get away; he's going to kill you; don't go near him.' But Magnus walked right up to him with no hesitation and put his hand on Claude's shoulder."

Maggie dabs the new oil on Phil's chest.

"But Magnus's hand, the one on Claude's shoulder – it looked like it was floating there instead of touching it. And he said to Claude, 'Don't worry. Don't say a word. I'm going to disappear. And Maggie and I will come back soon with a full set of oils. But don't say anything to upset Madame Peychaud. Don't tell her you did this. Tell her I did it. Maggie and I will make this right. But at a cost. And when you next hear from us, we're going to need you two to be strong and together.' Claude looked at him funny. Puzzled but trusting. Like he was an old friend from a forgotten planet. Then Claude laid down, Magnus cleaned up the mess, and we left."

Maggie dabs Phil's chest and rolls two fingers in a slow circle.

"And Magnus and I did get the oil collection back

126

together. And a production plan for the first commercial batch."

Phil stirs himself up a little. He speaks.

"We need to see Madame Peychaud again. We have to go tell her."

"I sent her a letter this morning. We couldn't tell her till we were ready. And I told her something else. You don't have to go see her. She will come to see you."

Phil falls back to rest in confusion. He watches her quietly close the shirt of his costume and put away the bottles. He dreams of a mime in a glass cube. Is it a memory or a dream? He and Magnus are back in grade school, watching a mime. No, the mime is not in a glass cube. He is in a bubble. He is pretending to be trapped. Fear fills the streets. Magnus reaches out a finger and pops the bubble. He turns to Phil, smiling.

"See?" he says.

Yes, it's like the bubble popped and all veils were cascading down so Phil could see with a new sharpness. But there was something more. The glass case. Leeza, oldest of the siblings, was reading to Phil from *Grimms' Fairy Tales*. He could not have been in grammar school yet. He could not read for himself. He just saw the lady in the glass case. Sleeping beauty. Trapped in the glass case. She looked at Phil with those eyes. Violet eyes. A knot of smooth black hair. A face nearby. In the room. Now seated and gazing at Phil up close.

"Elephant man, you have a secret, too."

It was Maggie. Phil felt his chest. The oils had rubbed in. He felt the slow pain of coming back up from the watery depths of the unconscious.

"I have a secret?" He is regaining traction in surface world, the real world. The room. Mardi Gras.

"Yes, your secret," says Maggie.

127

"When did you last see Magnus?" she asks.

Phil thinks for a minute.

"Oh, God." He remembers.

"It was the day of Hermia's art show. Gus and I met at the show. Hermia had taken off, and we were ... Oh, God." Phil hangs his head.

* * *

Gus sits on front steps of Phil and Hermia's apartment, kicking dirt at a small cactus.

* * *

"Go on," says the fairy queen. "Your secret."

"Gus was waiting at my house," Phil says.

"And I went back to the police station."

* * *

Phil sits in a conference room at the police station with two detectives.

* * *

Phil looks at Maggie earnestly.

"I see," Maggie says.

"What? What do you see? What was I supposed to do?"

Maggie looks at Phil thoughtfully. Phil hears a clock ticking somewhere. A very low ticking. Phil assumes it would be imperceptible had his senses not been heightened at the moment.

"I don't know," Maggie says.

The clock ticks.

"I know," Phil replies. "I shouldn't have betrayed my brother. I sent the cops after Magnus. I caused that car crash."

"What car crash?" asks Maggie.

Phil is starting to panic again. He speaks hesitantly, in fear that the response he gets will either belie his sanity or confirm Magnus's death. Ticking. He rubs his own chest.

"On TV."

He watches Maggie's eyes for a clue but there is nothing.

"The black corvette on TV," he continues. "Maybe I dreamed it. We were sitting at the bar at the Napoleon House…"

"Oh, *that* car crash," says Maggie abruptly. "No, you didn't dream it."

Phil wonders at her equanimity. Perhaps she too is insane.

"The car crash on TV," she continues. "A pity."

"Is that all you can say – a pity," says Phil in shock.

"What do you want me to say?"

"I want you to say, I want you to feel something. Feel what I feel. Magnus just …" He can't finish the sentence. He can say no more. He is suffering. Tormented. No, she cannot feel it. She feels nothing. His head hurts. Things are spinning. He feels his own suffering like a log on a fire. Suffering sticks. He is burning up all of his suffering sticks. Ashes. And from the ashes he will awaken in her some pity. He tries again, slowly, methodically.

"You just watched Magnus crash his car, and …"

"No I didn't."

129

"But … but …" His resolve is breaking again.

"That wasn't Magnus," she says.

"The black corvette," Phil repeats, trying to make sense of it. How could it not be Magnus?

"They released the name," she says. "The driver was Gerard Naquin."

Phil processes as quickly as his brain can process.

"Lil' Naquin?!" he says.

He sits up, but he is still confused.

"Lil' Naquin! That cop's nephew! The other black corvette! He almost killed me!"

Maggie, assuming Phil delirious, gives him a drink of water. She gently pushes him back down.

"Now," she says. "This time it will burn a little."

She pours a drop of oil from one of the Egyptian bottles into her hand. Then another drop from another bottle. The aromas are strong. Too strong, Phil thinks. Filling the room. Pungent, sharp. Flooding the room. *It is too much,* Phil thinks.

She rubs his torso. Upward from the solar plexus to the chest and toward the neck. The room fills with cedar and something else and burning.

"I had a dream," she says.

"Long ago, as a child. I had not met you or Magnus. It moved me, this dream. Maybe you've had the same dream."

Phil is intrigued at the novelty of her suggestion. He struggles to stay awake. Or to dream, or to lose himself in Maggie's dream. Or the dream of Maggie. It was all flowing together. He opens his eyes. To ground himself. But the room is not the room, and he is not in bed. He is walking with Maggie outdoors. She is younger, twenty maybe, robust with health. There is a wooded area and a pond. They are in a hollow sloped with green forests.

"We talked about you," Maggie says, laughing, more dancing than walking. "How you were stuck. He loves you, you know."

Phil smiles. "Yeah, I know."

It is all so strange. Laughing, smiling, looking at his life without trauma, without anxiety.

They sit by the pond. Phil lies back, feels the sun. Burning. Wonderful feeling of the hot sun on skin.

"Do you know about my dreams?" Maggie says.

"I figured," Phil replies.

It is so peaceful here.

"I saw you and Magnus and the mime," Maggie says.

"Yeah, that's my dream," Phil says, as if her presence in his dream – or his memory – were the most natural and obvious thing in the world.

"I know about the girl in the glass case," Maggie says.

"I figured," Phil replies, feeling the warmth, looking up at the tree branches extending out over the pond.

"I'm going to get you out," she says.

"Ok."

"For Magnus," she adds.

"Ok." Phil is too comfortable to ask questions. Question and answers seem oddly irrelevant. Then one question arises.

"Why did Magnus say he killed you?"

"Oh that? I told him to say that."

She tosses her dark hair and laughs.

Phil laughs too. And then he goes under.

* * *

131

"I always knew my life would be short." Maggie gurgled the words a little, as if she were chewing on something and speaking at the same time.

"But I didn't mind. It felt right. My mother, I am told, had the same problem – like a burning of coals in the mouth and throat. They say I learned things from my mother, but I don't know how. Maybe it's in the blood.

"I had stopped treatment, you know. I was dying. I was in my bed dying. I felt my heart stop. First there was the steady beat, like the ticking of a clock. And then there was nothing.

"'I knew my life would be short,' I repeated out loud. Or at least it seemed out loud to me.

"And then Magnus walked in. He had a box. An empty cake box. My name – or one of my names – was on it. But there was nothing in the box.

"Magnus could see that I was dead.

"'No,' he said.

"But I was gone. Gone, I remembered something from *The Tibetan Book of the Dead*.

...the soft white light of the gods, the soft red light of the jealous gods, the soft blue light of human beings, the soft green light of the animals, the soft yellow light of the hungry ghosts, and the soft smoky light of hell-beings. These six will shine together with the pure wisdom lights. At that moment do not grasp or be attracted to any of them, but stay relaxed in a state free from thought.

"And remembering it was the same as it being real. And so it was real. But Magnus walked in. And I grasped the soft blue light. One more cycle. I was back for

132

one more cycle. A brief cycle in the body. Four weeks.

"'I need you to help me,' I told Magnus. 'A difficult task.'

"Magnus was unquestioning.

"'First, Phil,' Magnus told me.

"'Yes. And Hermia too.' I said. Maybe Hermia too was sleeping in her glass case here. She was set to go to Laura's, Magnus could see that. But he could also see she was headed for spiritual trouble. Spiraling down. So he went with her. Get her settled. Keep the emotional crisis manageable."

* * *

Phil awakes, or seems to awake, and challenges Maggie.

"What about me? What about *my* emotional crisis?"

"What about you?" asks Maggie, surprised.

"Magnus took off and left me here," says Phil.

"You didn't need Magnus. He knew I was here."

"You!" exclaimed Phil. "You never even saw me."

"Turns out I didn't need to. You had Gus, you know."

Phil ponders for a moment.

"Wait," he says. "Who is Gus?" He asks it like he is trying to plot the characters, including himself, into some larger-than-life drama.

"Gus is your friend," she says.

That sounds somehow too mundane, too untranscendental to satisfy Phil.

"OK, Gus is my friend now, but didn't that seem a little shaky when Magnus took off with Hermia? Gus

133

wasn't my friend then." He feels a little bit of the old pettiness creeping back in.

"What do you mean?" asks Maggie. "Gus was always your friend. How can you not see that?"

She looks at him and he feels small under her gaze.

Phil's head hurts. His nostrils and eyes burn. But he persists.

"Why now? Why all of this now?"

"Because my time is up," Maggie says. The abrupt shift to her situation seems jarring for a second, then natural. Of course, all of our fates are entwined.

"And I need you too," she adds.

"*You* need *me*?" Phil asks in disbelief.

"Rites of passage. One stage to the next. You're at a passage moment right now, if Magnus has anything to say about it. And I'm at one for sure."

It hit home for Phil. She was dead. Or dying. Or passing. Whatever it was.

She rubbed his chest.

"You're getting me ready," she says. She looks around the room. "All of this is getting me ready."

"But…" Phil is at a loss for words. He feels a little as he did when he met Madame Peychaud.

"But Magnus …" No, he cannot figure out how to complete the sentence, the thought.

"Where is Magnus?" he says.

"He left something for you. It's in these boxes."

Phil notices several boxes at the side of the bed.

"Where is he?"

"He, he …"

Maggie's voice breaks and she picks up and once again uses the electronic larynx.

"A difficult task," says the electronic box.

134

"What task?" says Phil, animated. "Where is he?"

"On the way to India," says the box.

Maggie walks to the balcony and leans back against it. The sound of Mardi Gras revelers washes up from the street.

Phil tries to think.

"India?" he says.

He speaks louder so Maggie can hear.

"Magnus can't go to India! You even said yourself we're all connected. All the rings of the tree are still here. You said it yourself."

Maggie lingers against the balcony for a moment. She comes back in. She picks one of the red chrysanthemums from the vase and toys with it.

"Yes," she says. "The rings are here. Always. But they only become visible. When the tree falls."

At the decisiveness of the last word, Phil begins to panic again. Wait, he thinks. India is not only a metaphor. It's a place. A real place. He is like a detective now, trying to figure out the world in a way that makes it conform to his wishes.

"So, Maggie Leblanc, why is Magnus traveling in India, anyway?" he asks cleverly.

"He is going to see my father," she says point blank. Her otherworldly delivery knocks Phil back to insecurity. He falls back, eyes closed. He opens them, confused to see the fairy queen masked again. Her masked face seems aglow. Phil's own voice seems removed from himself.

"Who are you?" he asks.

She smiles at the novelty, the innocence of the question.

"The fairy queen."

Phil looks down despairingly at the boxes.

135

"What am I supposed to do with...? Didn't he say anything?"

"He said, 'Do this in memory of me.'"

Phil sinks back, eyes closed, trying to think, to think.

Do this in memory of me.

Phil looks up, doesn't see Maggie, sits up, sees her on the balcony, facing the crowd. She turns and leans back on the balcony. She holds the red chrysanthemum at her breast. She looks at Phil with those violet eyes, warm and full and deep, searching him for something, giving him something. Phil looks down, reaches with effort from the bed to the boxes. He picks up the top box and reads the inscription:

TO MY BROTHER
WHO WILL BE READY FOR THIS
WHEN HE RECEIVES IT

Phil looks back to the balcony, but it is empty.

Chapter 12

A funeral procession ends in an old New Orleans cemetery crowded with above ground stone vaults. The vaults are topped with mournful Christian imagery – crosses, angels drooped in tears, cherubs too woeful for their baby faces. The procession, though, abounds with icons of various religions and New Age groups. A priest's voice is faintly audible.

"*Requiem aeternam dona eis, Domine*. Grant her eternal rest, O Lord."

A slot to one of the vaults is freshly carved:

Maggie Leblanc 1970-1999

Gus and Phil, who are among the group, bow their heads. Phil is shaky, fresh from the bed and weak. Gus supports him. The priest walks away, past the cracked headstones toward the moss-laden oaks and cypress trees at the perimeter of the cemetery. Perhaps his concern for all souls has brought him here but his better judgment has him scurrying away before anything pagan breaks in on the divine spectacle.

The voodoo priestess stands and speaks.

"Close your eyes and feel, feel this city of the dead come to life to help our sister cross over. The city of the dead is come to life and we are but its shadows."

Gus whispers to Phil.

"This is definitely not like my aunt's funeral in New York. The cities of the dead here feel like they might really come to life."

A raspy, middle-aged woman's voice hammers down from behind.

"What you mean, 'might come to life'? You must be blind as a bat. Look around you and what do you see? Flesh and blood and spirit mixing and churning."

They turn and see Madame Peychaud.

"Madame Peychaud?!" Phil exclaims.

"Where the hell did you come from?" adds Gus.

"Got a letter from poor little Maggie. She told

me when and where to come. Always directing things, even from the city of the dead. She said y'all had the essential oils business all ready."

Gus and Phil look at each other confused.

"Yeah," Phil says. "Yeah, sure, we're ready. I just, we don't actually have the oils."

Madame Peychaud holds up a key.

"I got the key to the oils, you damned fool. I just need the shop space."

The conversation continues as they walk out of the cemetery.

"Yeah, sure, we got shop space at the Center. We're looking for new things to work with."

Phil hears his own voice echo off the cemetery's iron gate. He is speaking to Madame Peychaud, looking at her. Perhaps he'd never seen her in a dress, never seen her exposed to the shoulder. And the echo – and what he sees – captivates him. For a second, he ponders in sheer curiosity, trying to remember where he had seen it before. He is still speaking to Madame Peychaud but he doesn't know what he is saying. Where had he seen it before? And suddenly he knows. His mouth dries out. He knows where he saw it. The tiny rose tattoo on the caramel skin of Madame Peychaud's shoulder. But he is too frail from his Mardi Gras ordeal. He drops.

Someone is being carried. Someone is carrying. A white man being carried. A black man carrying. Other characters populate the scene. They are going down a street. Phil feels that he is somewhere in the scene but he doesn't know where. Is he the white man being carried? The black man doing the carrying? One or all of the others? Or is he the trees, the sun, the stucco facades, the atmosphere itself. He floats into the atmosphere. Up, up

138

he floats, surveying the scene below – a black man carrying a white man with a huddle of people moving along with them down the street. He is on top of a cathedral. The mime is there, on top of the cathedral. The bells ring.

"Wake up, baby." The voice is Madame Peychaud's.

Phil is back in the fairy queen's bedroom.

"Where are we?" Phil ventures. "Why are we …"

"Hush, baby. We don't have to be out of this room just yet."

Phil is still groggy. Everything seems symbolic.

We don't have to be out of this room just yet.

He starts to dream again. He is back in the hollow, at the pond with Maggie. She is young and beautiful.

"Do you know about my parents?" she is saying.

Phil doesn't answer. He is lying in the grass, feeling the sun, watching the leaves waver overhead, hearing the occasional "plip … plip" of a fish jumping in the pond.

"Once upon a time, I thought that he too betrayed a loved one."

Strange, Phil thinks. This conversation. Viewing our lives with such calm. Feeling the truth of things, but from a distance. Detachment. Compassion. They only work together. That's where he got it wrong. That's where people get it wrong. They think detachment and compassion are opposites. No, they are brothers, sisters, twins, always together. They only work together. Unconditional love means never missing anyone. If you miss them, your love is tainted by attachment, interest, possessiveness. As long as you're capable of missing someone your love is conditional. It's like a veil was lifted for Phil. He is getting excited. And his excitement breaks the spell. He looks at Maggie but the scene is fading, dissolving. Someone is standing across the room. Someone with her back to Phil. She is rinsing out a small towel in the sink. He hears Madame Peychaud's voice.

"This wild goose chase you been on the last few weeks, hunting around like that. It isn't really about Hermia, is it?"

"No ma'am. It's about Magnus."

Did he really say that? *No ma'am*? Is he a child again? No, he is just disoriented. He gathers his thoughts.

"I guess that's all I was thinking about for the past month. Why would Magnus do it?"

"Do what?" snaps Madame Peychaud.

"Kill Maggie Leblanc"

"What made you think he killed Maggie Leblanc?"

"He said so."

"Oh is that all?" Madame Peychaud says with a smile. "Because Magnus said so."

Phil thinks.

"This isn't about Magnus either, is it?" he says.

She shakes her head. Phil continues.

"It's about me."

"Now you getting somewhere, baby. I'm gonna have to hire you to be my fortune teller back at the shack. I just sit back and collect the money. You damn near partly right now."

"What do you mean, 'partly right'?"

"I mean you still got to get the other part."

"What other part?"

"It ain't just about you. It's about the Sunspot and Gus and Mary Elizabeth."

"Mary Elizabeth?"

"Yeah, baby. It's mainly about Mary Elizabeth."

"Mainly?"

"Look at you! You finally free of that damn job, you ain't got Hermia to lay there and die with every day, you don't know where the hell you going, and suddenly it's all about you."

"You just said…"

"Shush now!"

Madame Peychaud turns and places the hot, wet towel on his forehead. He collapses back to the pillow from the excess heat of the towel.

"Jesus!" he says.

She ignores his discomfort and continues.

"You just laying the groundwork. The world just gotta cleanse you so you can lay the groundwork."

"You mean Magnus gotta cleanse me."

"Yeah, I suppose that's part of why he told you he killed Maggie. Part of why he went off with Hermia. Get you to shake off the dust. Good for Hermia too."

"What about Maggie?" he asks.

"Maggie don't need no help.

"So she's at that level? The level Magnus was reaching for?"

"Yeah, she's at that level. Also, she dead."

"Dead?! But you just said …"

"Baby, baby, you saw her go off the balcony, didn't you? You was in the room."

It's true. How could he have forgotten? He had seen her on the balcony. Then not on the balcony. He was at her funeral, for Christ's sake.

But there was something else. Something Madame Peychaud had missed. Maggie had asked for help. First from Magnus, then from Phil. Yes, she was at that level, but she must still be part of the chain.

"*I need you to help me,*" she had said.

Help and be helped. All moving together.

But she had said it with compassion. Did that change things? Did it change the meaning of things? A familiar voice broke in on his incomplete reverie.

"When Magnus found out about her condition," Madame Peychaud went on. "Maggie with one foot in the grave, I imagine that got the ball rolling for him and he come to wake you up."

"But why did Magnus have to .... What did she mean, he's gone to see her father? Is Magnus dead or not?"

"Sometimes hard to say if people's dead or not. We like to think it's one or the other but lots of people's in between. Some of the people we call dead is still with us. Some we call living ain't no more alive than Napoleon and Josephine. The line between the spirit world and the flesh ain't never been so straight as we want it."

"Where is Magnus?" asks Phil, becoming more alert and getting tired of the circumlocution.

"OK, OK, hold your horses. You never can say for sure about Magnus – if you could he wouldn't be Magnus – but ..."

"Get to the point!" says Phil, with an authority equal to Madame Peychaud's. This seems to focus Madame Peychaud, and from this point forward she speaks directly, eye-to-eye.

"Maggie's earthly father is in Goa, India. Took the Hippie Trail from Istanbul."

"Why didn't he take Maggie?"

"He didn't know about Maggie. Not till a few weeks ago."

Madame Peychaud is squirming now,

uncomfortable in a way that Phil would never have imagined possible. Now he is the interrogator and she the witness.

"How do you know this and he doesn't?"

Madame Peychaud was gasping. No, sobbing. Sobbing gently.

"My fault, my fault."

Phil softens.

"It seems like everybody's got a secret."

Madame Peychaud regains composure.

"Her father, Ziggy was his hippie name, the only name I ever knew. He run out on the draft to Montreal in 1970. Draft-dodging was illegal, but not too big a deal. But they got a big warrant for him on hard drugs and racketeering."

"Oh, my god," says Phil, head in hands.

"It was all bogus of course, all because of a hippie dreamer kid called Ragman with a vision for changing the world. Yeah, the more vision he had, the more the cops hated him. Right to hate him, too, because he *could* have changed the world. So, yeah, LSD and drugs was part of the shake-up, part of the breaking free and breaking down of the old ways of seeing. So they killed Ragman in a drug bust and put Ziggy next on the list."

"Back to the point, Madame Peychaud. No one needs the story of everyone who ever lived. Get back to the point."

"The point is, I was the only one who knew Ziggy's whereabouts when he took off, and I didn't tell him about Maggie. I knew he'd come back, and I knew they'd get him. The old system fighting against the hippies was strong. They was scared. They'd a killed Ziggy in one, two, three, 'cause he too had vision. He didn't know it so much as Ragman but the forces fighting

143

against change knew it intuitively. Ziggy was what the new man was going to be, free from all their conventions and material traps, free to love one another for real. So I never told him."

"What about Maggie's mother. She must have known."

"Ah, Jazmine," Madame Peychaud said, closed her eyes and looked back. "She was something."

Jazmine," Phil cut in. "From the psyc ward."

Madame Peychaud looked at him strange.

"Yeah, she was in. She didn't belong in, but they had her in for a little while. Shocked she was, that was all. Too much power that girl had. See things more than I could see things. She knew secrets from the forests nobody else knew. Old wisdom. Even she don't know how she had it."

"What happened to her?"

Madame Peychaud's jaw tightened.

"Died in childbirth. Another story that was. We were living on a hippie commune – the real deal – in Dutchess County, New York. We were all from here. Louisiana. New Orleans. Lil swamp towns. But cops in those days wasn't so good for people like us. We had a big blowout at the old iron works and had to get out of town. Ended up at that commune in Dutchess. Then Jazmine died and it sent a shock wave. Some people said she died because she had the baby at the commune, and it was all midwives and natural medicine. No hospital. It's true there was no hospital. I don't know if it would a made a difference. But that was the beginning of the end of that beautiful commune. It just frayed out from there. We lasted a few more years. Never see a dream like that in real life again. People really living for each other outside the system. But anyway, I told Ziggy Jazmine died and

144

weren't nothing to be done about it. That's all he needed to know. Then I heard he hit the Hippie Trail from Istanbul to Goa, India."

"So Magnus ..." started Phil.

"I don't know nothing about no Magnus," said Madame Peychaud sharply, back in character.

Chapter 13

It took Phil a while to settle back into his old apartment. He felt like an interloper in someone else's world. But now his strength is restored, and he surveys the room as his own. He begins to take the contents out of the boxes he received from Magnus through Maggie. They hold many spring-clip bound manuscripts. He flips through, viewing the title pages of the first few:

> *The Four Sheaths and Levels of Abstraction*
>
> *Adversity and Abundance*
>
> *Imagination, Reason, and the Spiritual Vortex*
>
> *The Akashic Record and the Concept of Time*

"Hey, Gus!" Phil calls out.

"Come here!"

Gus comes from the other room in a plaid robe with coffee.

"Look here, Gus. There must be 10, 12, 15 different manuscripts here."

"Damn!" is all Gus says.

"What are we going to do with all this?" asks Phil.

Gus shakes his head.

"He must have given this to you for a reason."

Madame Peychaud now enters from the kitchen.

"Lotta people would kill for those."

"You think?" says Phil. "Two weeks ago, you would have killed Magnus without these."

"Still might kill him, if I ever see him. But that doesn't matter now. Every quack, guru, and seeker from Southern California to Upstate New York heard of Magnus. Mm-mm."

She chuckles.

"That boy never missed a conference and always made an impression."

She fingers the manuscripts as one might an antique ceramic doll.

"These gonna need some messing with. Can one of you fools edit a manuscript?"

"Can one of you fools?!" repeats Phil, aspirating.

"Of course, I can edit. You think I can't edit?"

Phil calms down and thinks for a second.

"But then what?"

"Then you sell them. Save the world and give yourself a damned job."

"How we gonna sell them?"

Madame Peychaud and Phil contemplate briefly.

"Come on, guys," Gus exclaims in disbelief.

"Can I sell shit? You think I can't sell shit?"

They snicker at Gus's salesman bravado.

"Get ready, y'all," says Madame Peychaud.

"This is big. Everybody knows Magnus. If you pull this off, your little store's going to be a magnet for holy men and wingnuts, and you not gonna be able to tell the difference."

"Can you tell the difference?" asks Phil seriously, recalling one of Magnus's lectures, slipping into a childlike curiosity.

Madame Peychaud looks at him indignantly. Gus catches her glare and teases her.

"Isn't this where you're supposed to slap a sign and say, 'Of course I can tell the difference'?"

Madame Peychaud looks at Gus glumly.

"There is no difference."

"Well, why bring it up?"

Madame Peychaud looks at Gus as though at a tenderfoot in a dangerous work zone. After a moment of glowered pity, she gives him a nod and straightens her chin.

"Deep down, there ain't no difference. But we gotta work this plane too. We gotta keep the top connected to the bottom. You youngsters gonna need to keep old Madame Peychaud around for a while."

* * *

Phil and Madame Peychaud are in the courtyard of the Napoleon House, thick with palms, squared by apricot stucco walls and wrought-iron balconies.

"What about the picture in the newspaper?" Phil asks.

"It was you. I saw the tattoo."

"Yeah, it was me."

"But the child?"

"That lil baby was Maggie. They got that right."

147

"Your daughter?"

"No. They got that wrong. My daughter was the other one, the bigger one. She was in the picture, too, if you open your damn eyes and look."

"You have a daughter?!"

"Yeah, I have a daughter."

"Why didn't you say so?"

"Nobody asked. She been traveling a couple years. We talk every now and then. But she's busy. You know how kids are."

"Yeah," Phil says. Funny, he thinks. Me sitting here with Madame Peychaud commiserating about those damn kids in their twenties. Like finding a seat at the table that someone's been holding for you.

"So you raised her and Maggie together."

"Yeah. Like sisters."

"No wonder you were so sensitive when you thought Magnus was wrecking your oils business." Phil smiled.

"Sensitive about Magnus because Magnus sometimes a damn fool."

"I thought you said he was the great sage who was going to pull in gurus and seekers from around the world," said Phil slyly.

"You can be a great sage and a damn fool at the same time," she snapped. "Magnus proof of it."

"I think you're a little jealous, Madame Peychaud." Phil chuckled, and imagined Madame Peychaud chuckling beneath her stoic expression.

"What's her name?" he asks. "Your real daughter."

"Rose Petal."

* * *

Several weeks have passed. Phil stands on a ladder painting the front exterior of the Center. Mary Elizabeth approaches in her new, red Easter dress. Leeza follows.

"Uncle Phil! Uncle Phil!" Mary Elizabeth cries. "You want some chocolate?"

"No, honey. I'm working."

"It's from France," she adds, partly in pride and partly in generosity, as a way of enhancing the temptation.

Phil steps down a rung, takes a piece, and closes his eyes.

"Mmm. He says. I see a castle sprawling across a field in southern France. Mmm. Now I see the Eiffel Tower. Now I see the Notre Dame cathedral. I see the gargoyles on top, in the bell tower. Wait! Now there's a princess there!"

"Is it me?" cries Mary Elizabeth. "Am I the princess?"

"Hmm, let me see," Phil says. He scrunches his eyes tighter.

"Yes! It's Princess Mary Elizabeth!"

Mary Elizabeth is delighted to be in the story, but as a princess she cannot help but see herself in the third person."

"Is the princess in the bell tower?"

"Yes, and the bells begin to ring. Bong. Bong. Bong."

Phil rocks his head with each "bong." Mary Elizabeth attends, serious.

"The gargoyles. Now they are whispering."

Mary Elizabeth is amused but concerned.

"Are they trapped in the bell tower?"

"Yes, they're whispering about how to get out. 'Let's go this way.' 'No, that way.'"

"Is the princess trapped?"

Phil can see the gradient in Mary Elizabeth's expression slide further toward the "concerned" end. He remembers his own concern when Leeza had read to him from "Sleeping Beauty."

"Yes, but only for a time," Phil says. "It's the princess who finds the way out."

"What's the way out?"

"Well, one of the gargoyles, the fattest one, was blocking a tiny little door."

"How tiny?"

"Tiny enough to be blocked by the fattest little gargoyle."

Mary Elizabeth's face turns to consternation at this tautological knot.

"But how did they get out?"

"Well, the princess poked the little gargoyle in the belly, and he wobbled and fell over, exposing the tiny door for all to see."

Mary Elizabeth is all eyes.

"The gargoyles, who were smaller than a human child, tumbled through the tiny door and rumbled down the stone passageway."

"What about the princess?"

"The princess squeeeeezed through the door …"

Here Phil squeezes Mary Elizabeth gently on both sides, lifting and jiggling her around until she breaks through to laughter. Then he sets her down and continues.

"And she never got trapped again in the bell tower or any place else in that big old cathedral ever

150

again."

Mary Elizabeth laughs, then becomes serious again.

"Did you see the hunchback?" she queries with eyes wide.

"No. Must be in the next bite."

Mary Elizabeth eagerly takes the next bite and closes her eyes. Phil goes back to work, paints a few strokes, nearly falls off the ladder, regains composure, dips the brush, hears a rugged male voice.

"Eh-yeee! Get down here, cher! You better let a man do dat paint!"

Phil turns and smiles to see Mr. Claude.

"Hey, Mr. Claude! What's the matter? You don't think I'm a man?"

"Not yet. But you getting dere. Now get down here wit your family."

Phil descends and Mr. Claude scampers up with a sure foot. Phil's cell phone rings.

"Hello … hey, Hermia, how are you?!"

"Good, good," she says.

"You got a cell phone?!" Phil says.

"No," Hermia says. "This is Laura's phone. I moved in with her."

"You moved in with Laura?!"

"Yeah, I went back to college. I'm going to get my Fine Arts degree."

"Back to college? Well, that's, that's a great idea. How are you getting around?"

"Magnus gave me the corvette."

"Magnus did what?"

"Yeah, he said consider it repossessed by someone that needed it."

"The corvette," says Phil in wonder. "No

151

kidding. Yeah, he gave me something, too."

"Really? Well, hey, Phil, maybe you can come to the art show at the end of the semester in May."

"Yeah, I'd like that. I'd really like that."

"OK, Phil, stay in touch."

"You, too, Hermia."

Phil hangs up and stares into space in momentary reverie. His trance is interrupted by Mary Elizabeth.

"Uncle Phil! Uncle Phil! Gus is here!"

Gus approaches in a new suit with a suitcase and a bouquet of white chrysanthemums.

"Hey, Gus," says Phil. "How was New York?"

"Big and bad as usual."

Mary Elizabeth runs up and hugs Gus.

"Hey, it's the little queen!"

"I'm not a queen. I'm a princess!"

"A princess! Well, lucky for us. I have a special flower that grew and grew and grew …"

Gus picks through the chrysanthemums looking for the most perfect one.

"… as a special gift …"

He draws a beautiful white chrysanthemum from the bouquet.

"… just for a princess."

He gives her the flower. She turns it over in her hand and studies it, as if she sees something no one else sees. Gus loops a shell necklace over her head.

"From Coney Island," he says.

The necklace reminds her of something. Something she felt when she bit into that chocolate, losing herself in the dream of the hunchback. She feels the first ache of responsibility in her life. But with the ache is a sense of power.

Phil sees the expression on Mary Elizabeth's young face. He knows now what Madame Peychaud meant.

It's mainly about Mary Elizabeth.

Phil follows Mary Elizabeth's gaze, distant, then turning to Gus. Yes, Gus. Phil almost forgot.

"Any luck, Gus?" asks Phil.

"Luck on what?"

"Come on, the publishing houses."

"Oh, the publishing houses."

Gus looks down despondently. He hands Phil a letter. Phil takes the negative cue as he opens the letter.

"Shit!"

Gus smiles gently at his own little joke. Phil begins to read and is pleasantly surprised.

"That's just the advance?!" Phil asks.

"Just the beginning. They want a contract on the next four."

"Damn, Gus!"

Phil and Gus look at each other, not sure what to do next. Gus turns serious and asks Phil a question.

"Can I sell shit?"

Their excitement bursts out.

"Yes, you can sell shit! Damn, Gus, you can sell shit!"

Mr. Claude has come down off the ladder and stands arm-in-arm with Madame Peychaud.

"Dat boy can sell shit, eh Storm-Cherie?"

"Yeah, Claude. Knuckle head, but he can sell shit for sure. He's got a lucky charm for selling shit."

Gus takes issue in mock-pomposity.

"No charm, m'lady, no magic at all. Just the

153

science of rhetoric."

"You hear that, Cherie?" pipes in Claude. "Dat boy got a silver tongue for rhet-rick."

Mary Elizabeth and Leeza have set up a small picnic table with snacks and the flowers. All amble toward the table.

Madame Peychaud responds to Claude's encomium on Gus's talented parts. "He better watch that tongue! I'll take that charm right off his ass!"

Gus takes Madame Peychaud's arm on the other side from Mr. Claude, and the three continue toward the table, arm in arm.

"No hexes, now, Madame Peychaud," says Gus. We're in business together now, you and I."

She gives him a look.

"Bunch of damned fools I'm in business with."

The angle widens to show the full, freshly painted sign across the wellness center, scrolling above the heads of the picnickers:

L U N A R   L A N D I N G

WELLNESS CENTER

THE END

Epilogue

A monkey swaggers on a flat rooftop. Smells patch into a prayer quilt of sorts – cow dung, incense, Asian spices being cooked into rice. A haggard old man sits cross-legged. He can see a tea shop, a palm tree, and a small Hindu shrine, like a half-height phone booth, shining red and gold and light blue, as if awaiting some astral transmission. A row of squat buildings, stain-streaked stone walls, stretches out from his field of vision.

The old man finishes his meditation, stands, stretches. He does not look haggard when he stands. His shirtless torso is strong like a tree trunk, his mane of gray hair black-streaked and pulled back to a bun. His pants are light, lemon-colored, baggy, and seem to float. He rarely goes down to Arjuna Beach in Goa any more. Not like the old days. The days when everything was new and there were no rules – just the sound of the sea, the sand, the silver moon, and the sad cry of the gulls. There was always the sad cry of the gulls. But that was part of it. The land of inner discovery. Local girls would come to giggle at the hippies. They would smoke a little pot. Life was good. The beach was more of a club scene now. The old man would go once in a while to see the kids dancing. He liked to see them dance. But something was missing.

Last Wednesday he went to the weekly flea market. He had heard about a new American in town. There were lots of Americans in Goa, but this one was different, searching for something, combing other villages – Batim and Ponda and Tiswadi. He seemed like a ghost to the locals, passing between the fish vendors and silk merchants and artisans, in and out of kiosks and copper shops. But he was more than a ghost, and he apparently knew the old man's habits. At a tea shop off the main road, where swamis and swindlers hunched over steaming green and black teas and masala chai, and gossipers gathered with teeth red from betel nuts, the old man sat awaiting the brew he had sipped off and on at this particular shop for years. The American had been here. Another patron, another old man, with a broad white beard and smiling eyes and a peach-colored turban, approached. Yes, the American. Where was he? Gone. Faded into the jungles of central India. To live or die there as anyone knows. On his own inscrutable journey. But the old man. The man with the peach-colored turban and smiling eyes. A message was delivered. "For Ziggy," the old man had said.

Now Ziggy stands in his own village, stretches again his shirtless torso, smooths his baggy lemon pants. He has not crossed the ocean in many years, but he has little to pack: a few shirts, a toothbrush. He does not know what he will find. But he must go. In memory of the daughter he never knew he had.

* * *

Mary Elizabeth stands at the foot of the ladder, tastes the chocolate Uncle Phil had returned to her before he ascended the ladder to continue painting. Sweet with a little bitter. Her eyes scrunch. She is in the cathedral. She searches for the hunchback. Large stone rooms, small nooks with narrow windows. Through tunnels and down spiral stairwells. Down,

down. In a damp, dark underchamber, with just a little light filtering down from above, she sees another figure. A wanderer he seems, gray hair flowing in a wild mane. He wears a necklace of rudraksha beads, like little walnuts, bumpy and grooved, Lord Shiva's teardrops.

"I'm looking for the hunchback," Mary Elizabeth says.

"And who is the hunchback?"

"He is … everyone thinks he's ugly but he saves the princess. He saves everybody."

"And where have you looked for this hunchback?"

"I've been through tunnels and stairs, in the bell tower, I don't know where else."

The old man smiled.

"You know," Mary Elizabeth said. "You know, don't you?"

"Yes."

"Can you tell me the way?"

"You are the way."

***

A streetcar rolls through mid-city New Orleans on a wide street lined with oaks. A young woman newly returned is among the riders. She has much to think about. Her travels have been fruitful. She has learned much. Now she is back and energized but without direction. She will soon meet those who will be family to her. She pulls out a skeleton key and plays her fingers along it. Little does she know that the man from India will be there. She will remember him. The tall, sweet man, he who gave her the skeleton key when she was a child.

***

At the cemetery at the end of Canal Street, the spirits rest in their little stone houses, some with cracked faceplates, some tilting this way and that. Gathered around Maggie's grave is the company that has bonded so well since the grave was first marked – Madame Peychaud and Mr. Claude, Phil and Gus, Leeza and Mary Elizabeth. One by one, they drop a flower in front of the stone tomb. Mary Elizabeth goes last. She says a prayer in her own fashion and then turns away from the tomb. Her young eyes see further than anyone present. She sees a woman approaching on the streetcar. One who will join them and live at the Sunspot. Yes, the Sunspot. When Mr. Claude and Madame Peychaud moved down to help at the Lunar Landing, they found a property with three cottages and a shared yard, and all joined in. It was Mary Elizabeth who insisted on calling it the Sunspot after the wellness center was renamed. So the young woman stepping down from the streetcar will join them as their little community strengthens.

And another Mary Elizabeth sees. A man with wild gray hair pulled to a bun. He arrives from far away. He has not seen this place in many years. He would not live with them but would settle in the bayou country nearby. He would visit often. He is close to Madame Peychaud and remembers Rose Petal as a little girl. He has many stories to tell, and with each his own strength seems restored. Mary Elizabeth is his keenest audience. She feels as though she knows him from another time. And when he is gone, she knows

158

instinctively that he will be watching from a distance, from a shack out on the bayous, pouring his spirit into the community, he guiding her and she guiding him through the next pass.

* * *

Please take a minute to go to Amazon and leave an honest book review. Reviews help me as the author and help steer prospective readers to books they like.

Gary Gautier was born in New Orleans, has hitchhiked through 35 states and 16 countries, run two marathons, and once, due to a series of misadventures, spent six months as the chef at a French restaurant. He holds a Ph.D. and has taught university writing and literature. His publications include children's and scholarly books, novels, poetry, articles in peer-reviewed journals, and book reviews.

Selected books by Gary Gautier:

Hippies
In this Age of Aquarius epic, a group of hippies tossed between the ideals and the pressures of the late 1960s counterculture discover an LSD-spinoff that triggers past life regressions and leads them toward a dramatic climax.

Mr. Robert's Bones
Three kids awaken dark memories in an abandoned house and join with some old-timers to save the neighborhood from its own past. A family-friendly novel for ages 14 to adult.

Year of the Butterfly
In this chapbook of poems, two figures meet, cross landscapes and oceans, and part in a lyrical journey that is archetypal in scope but intimate in human connection.

Spaghetti and Peas
This beautifully illustrated hard-bound picture book brings a zany, heartwarming adventure to life for 3-8 year olds.

Contact   Web: www.garygautier.com
             Email: drggautier@gmail.com
             Blog: www.shakemyheadhollow.com

Made in the USA
Middletown, DE
15 July 2020